3 1336 00198 0730

D1106763

Nobody Called Me Mine

Nobody Called Me Mine

Black Memories

by Frederick Ward

Tundra Books 1977
Plattsburgh, N.Y.,

First printing.

Published in the United States by
Tundra Books of Northern New York
Plattsburgh, New York 12901
ISBN 0-912766-37-9
Library of Congress Card No. 75-44838

Published in Canada by
Tundra Books of Montreal
Montreal, Quebec H3G 1J6
ISBN 0-88776-067-8

Printed in the United States

To my brother James (1938 - 1976) and Robert

TABLE OF CONTENTS

Gull-Bird

The gull-birds shout out:

CALL OUT! Who's that

lying in the rain,

mouthing 'darknesses'

through pop'd saliva bubbles

Nobody Called Me Mine

'his yells and hollers went through they ears and

come'd out in whispers on they lips...'

MISS PEMBA

I fell and cut myselfs on a thorn
but it be your face that bleed
O the Lord, must mark us fer sure
to know us from our oneness;

Pemba Jade, be the age of yellowing photographs and slow movements, flip flying things bout the night lights and a *goneness* of what *were* when you only see'd its shadow —come'd—

A dark blue, wool saucer tam with the knot in the center, supported by an octagon base and grey every-which-a-way hair covered her head. Cepting fer her thick bifocals – rimmed in silver what extended her eyes out over her nose – and rouged-on mouth, the rest of her face be a testimony on blackness. She wore her no style blue green overcoat covering a long everyday dress – lacy black on shiny something – which hung to her old heavy black low heel nurse's shoe tops. She'd been shopping afore she come'd to the cemetery and what she couldn't put into her string shopping bag or in her purse, she bundled up in a brown paper sack to carry under her arm, *alternating.* Her walking sways be paced by an old cane and some days a raggidy dirt grey dog trailed her sniffing under her long dress and tho, the dog be in back or to the side of her, she'd always – in little quick jerks – flip-push her cane out front of her – never turning around – to shoo it away: 'GIT! away, damnit! '

In the cemetery, the dog'd go on ahead of her, sniffing at the grave stones and pissing on the flower reefs and such like. Pemba Jade, stepped farward to a stop-look-around motion, her right arm reaching and hand rest-ready pressed full onto a head stone – her head cocked in the sparrows' sight-look, til quicklike, she think she *seen:*

'...is that yours, Aaron...? ' which lefted her mouth open. Then, right erect, her fingers'd stand stiff; arched; — took on the pose of a alert but less-little-steady-aged, black hound, shaky and rhythm-sniffing out Old Aaron's grave from a top the leaning head stone. It's truth! The dirt grey dog come'd circle Miss Pemba Jade, searching fer attention NONE it ran on off, his tail slapping her dress and turning the air the swirls of, at her feet, just rose'd up without notice.

Miss Pemba, leaned up in the expectance, pulled her purse, string bag and brown paper sack to her breast til a heaviness come'd from not being sure — she squinted on the distance — to suredness: 'Darlin aint there...' closed her mouth to swallow and look in other directions: 'Aaron, you aint gots no wheres to go to! ' she asked from inquiring sweetness too tired to worry herselfs...she stooped to sag: 'Which be your place? ' and kneeled to sit, thinking that his being there in the grave yard. Enough.

She lost his grave fer sure that day.

Aaron, pressed his hands, soft, to
to the sides of Pemba Jade's face
...in this feeling they'd played
their be'gatherness day, nodded each other — like children —
into marriage and sought nothing
else from each other; in that the
full were always theirs

A amberness be in her eyes that'd peek a excitement in you even not, but yet no one caring of her were ever put to make words of or notions bout this *excitement;* this *touch of discovery* that'd

embrace your being when ever you see'd her from a far or passed,
'HELLOing' her maybe meeting her fer the first time

O to hold her hand

or, when the spirit let up on you, touch her giggle.

She were kind-dark.

Pemba Jade, thought on the first time she left him. Aaron throw'd her clothes iron at her after she'd told him: 'You be like a great cliff standing there in no need what so ever! even though the sea waves be mashed and scratching way at you. What place is there fer me beneath such stone of arrogance? ' Whew! and days later, Aaron be caught up in forgitfulness and amazement: 'Where that woman'd? Pemba Jade? '...poked his sunday cane bout the hedge and such, seeking her 'wheres' — she come'd home.

It werent no much too cold so she lifted her coat from bout her shoulders which fell to flowering round her waist and sittings; then pull-tucked the bottom round her knees and out stretched legs and looking into space, thought on what she could catch...The sun come'd and she seemed to relax more. Her bare fore arms be folded over elbos resting in eachs' hand — like great loaves of wheat dough twisted at the ends and rising on her stomach. She be rocking. Thinking.

sore-full eyes that
slides to the 'wheres'
even to touch his fingertip
be guided by its warmth

'Come on woman   find-it-touch the tip of me finger. Alright.
You seen it. Now close your eyes and touch the tip of it. Dont look.
That's it. Then touch your nose ...and I'll touch mines. Huh! Aint
that intimate? Do it gin.'

'Yes, let's'

*He'd stand his finger in the air afore him I'd conclude a fix on it
from the end of my nose — it make a funny face, you knows —
Then I'd raise my finger out tip-front and squinted on the distance.
Assured now, I'd then close my eyes and seek him out.*

'Find-it-touch
the tip of me finger.'

O it were some magic to find his print and some awe powerful to
bring that touch on back to myselfs, press approval on my nose
and open my eyes Lord! to see *THE FACE OF HIS SMILE!*

MUHP! would pop-part Pemba Jade's lips and she'd gesture a
'O well, shush off my lap' motion to nothingness.

*the loudest touch
yes! the body has
its ways of speaking
in giggles when it
wish*

'Well, that Aaron, he coming from off somewhere. O! He sweep
such dust over your eyes to scent up the surrounds —

'makes you heart to RARE HIGH!   yes, your mind to think: it
be the first moment of yourselfs; with sweet

'lies that gives you *gas* later from unsettlement in your whole selfs
when you finds   he be gone

'He left some hair bits in the comb on the toilet drain.'

Then she'd phew-sigh her breath past-tween her pouted lips and rest
back on her palms in the september yellow-brown grass.

Part I

Growing Up

...where I be left'd to myselfs most, I aint all that bad.

1. Aunt Lil and Uncle Nough

I, as remembers, lived mostly
always with aunts and uncles
or in care of some kind of help

I aint got no sayings
on my mama or papa
but I be holy birth
— that you can knows fer sure —
and I were born to where I is
caused I desired and asked
in the 'WHERES', fer to come'd here.

This I done on my own
ceptin fer my mama and papa
prayed fer a boy

Aaron Strutter

Mostly, to make some mercy fer myselfs, I tell this story. When there were moments to speak, I touch'd through, done'd my thoughts and tween them extremes I tried to tell what I meant. 'Reaching out's' what they calls it today. When I'd gits into trouble, the womens'd huddle and hug they breast in talk bout me as: 'he just funnin'... 'he be a very talented boy with no outlet fer them creations from within'... 'so, sort of in answer to the rage in him'... 'outragins, that be what cause him to do bad'...'he were a sweet child growing up' ...and whole lots of head nodding: *'right honey's'*, til touch-pat push-aways would satisfy them to keep on doing what they be doing, cept one dear soul — there's got to be one — would try to revive the backbiting with: 'Dont you know, his Uncle...' and butterflys of sound'd make you wave your both hands limp, from your face and turn your head from all that.

Aunt Lil, posses's a photo picture of Uncle Lew, — *done/and gone dancing* (they says, he become'd a habitual criminal) — and in candle light, at night when I be spose'd to be sleep, Aunt Lil'd, sneak ...tense-tip to tip-tense, tempt'd and bend, knee down next of on my pallet to hold that photo of Uncle Lew, near next of my face to see's if I ever gonna grow'd to looks of him; and with a pointed finger, to see's if she *can* imagize me grow'd up full to be habitual like him and I guess she caught in the candle flicker enough proof cause she always woke me up with her trembling: *'Wooo's* (and) *O, My. Ohoo's,'* so that afore long I could — were spose'd to — DO WRONG! cause 'it *be* his destiny' and I were 'boundaried to a quick, always-gonna-be END' in whispers of: 'I tol you's...'

UNCLE NOUGH got old couldnt not talk right no more. I got so many troublings after then. Once I use to go home and he'd help me to see things. I would take some talk to him and he'd sort of 'splain it to me.

When I be ten or eleven, I remembers one night a vision... I be laying in bed this night Uncle had gifted me with a beating that afternoon fer something that I thought I shouldnt been beat fer. So I got very mad at him and I told (him) I says to myselfs that I were going to do everything that be bad. I dont care what I do. I dont care I'm just gonna do it cause *he* dont want me to do it! That night I got into bed and I didnt say my prayers and that's something I always did. In the middle of the night I woke up. I be dreaming I be playing with the Evilest and he wanted me to do all these bad things. I kept telling him I says no no no. You just do this one good thing more with me and I'll do what ever you want me to do. So he says okay. Altho, I couldnt picture what he looked like in the dream, I be afraid but anxious. He says alright, one more good thing. You knows, the Evilest, will do good if he thinks you gonna go with him later; fer all time *'specially!*

But when he wanted me to do something bad, I woke up. I looked at the door of my room. There be a light on it which be wrong cause as the light always come'd through the window, that light really would shine on the head of my bed not on the door. I looked over at the door agin and there be a face on it laughin at me! I got nervous and my heart started beating hard. I covered my head over and started to pray. My sister were in the bed with me but she aint fer moving either. That face were still there. I covered my head agin and prayed: 'God, why dont You help me? You knows, make this thing go way.' But it wouldnt go way. Finally, I covered my head over agin and there be this burning in my ears and there come'd this voice says: 'There's a bible on his dresser   go open it and read it.' After that I got this courage   I got up out of the bed, I turned the light on and I run'd into my Uncle's room. But this time I be in tears. Sure enough, when I got to his room there be the big hard black-covered bible on his dresser. I be so scared and he were upset cause he didnt know'd why I be crying, that I just crawled into bed with him and I never know'd   I never bothered to open it and read it.

I often wondered after that what I would done read if I done open the book. After that I preached a lot to my fingers cause Uncle be the onliest one who believed me cepten my fingers.

I come'd to dinner one night and there were these turnips. I didnt like the look. I never tasted them first   just says: 'NO!   Aint want it'   Uppidy like   I clamped both my hands – one on the other – over my mouth, my feet swing-scizzoring the air neath tween the legs of my chair. 'My to God! '   O, Aunt Lil's face come'd right tropical. Her eyes filled some-crazy with heat and I most believes, she put her mouth right next of in my ear   says: 'Aaron?   You gonna eat them now!   or they gonna be served to you E-VE-RY-DAY til you do; even if they rots. You hears? '

O, my silence

I never un-clamped my mouth.

She then took them from the table...*did* put them in the ice box. I were defiant; swelled up and went right on to bed with nothing.

She echo'd: *'E-VE-RY-DAY, til you...you hears? '*

Damn right, in my dreams I heard it.

Next day, I went to the ice box and stood open the door looked at them turnips and cried on the thought of the could-I-ever-eat-them-taste. Everytime I come'd to the table, them turnips come'd be presented the same as the first time, tho not warmed over. Four days and nights I come'd and they come'd. Without words, turnips be all I be served at the table. I got down melancholy come'd with malady and *slow'd, unusual,* up to the table two nights straight. Yet, the sickness? it be in me a reason fer *pushing my fist* together, more. Stubborn, damn. Stubborn! My play, sometimes-hang-round-the-house-uncle, Uncle Nough, took up my cause, sneaking me food at the late evening hours aint says a word, just look me a shud-hush!

On the table of the fifth day, I seen some rot come'd and remembered my Aunt Lil's pledge, indeed it be five days of her deliberate's-ness; I believed I would lose eventually, *done;* to eat even the rot so I ate them afore they *really* got bad.

Twenty years later, I be in a place-stop where there only *be* turnips.

2. Tyrone

You sees
Tyrone?

Strutter'd miss him all his life.

You'd carry him like a sack-bag of somethings, so he got that name: Bag of Groceries. But I always called him, Tyrone. He were my friend. My sister, Charlesetta'd love that boy much. Just: '...love to chew on him' ...and she'd make them sock-loud suck sounds, kissing and biting on his cheeks, like she do. Tyrone'd giggle-curl-up just like a fuzzy walker worm'd do when you put press a stick on its anywheres.

That child would take a spider fer a ride! Spiders were Tyrone's *weakness* – that means his love itch. He'd always be showing a spider a good time; pushing them down slides, pulling them in all sorts of boxes tied to string; sent the things on sailings on the sea and such like that. Well, it were a time, he put a spider on a swing seat and spit cover-over it on the seat so it couldnt fall way. Then push swing high and stand back so it'd fly freely – singing the child magic tune he made and dance-laughing. But he'd take notice that the spider'd be all scrunched up! And the swing chains sometimes tends to git tangled up as they do since it aint be no weight on it. So Tyrone, holden the limp, squirmed up spider cupped up in his hand would swing with it out towards; higher and higher fer only the sun to see! trying to dry it out. Charlesetta'd love that boy so much. Just: '...love to chew on him.'

He always eat his way into sleep
and when the boy dont like the food
he go to sleep anyway, right at the table;
sweetness and light all week

They says of Tyrone, that he so quick with his fist that he could jab-hit a fly in the mouth in mid air while it be in flight and give it a big lip on itselfs. Yes, that and other such dreams he gonna be, when he be growd.

Martha and Will Baptist (Cree Indian folks living to the west), they says to his mama: 'As this child grow old, we wants to hear of it — yes, honey — let us knows how he done growd up so far. Course we dont reads so we aint expects no writing. Yet, Lord bless! Bound-us-connected through his years in this way: we'll full know, if you be pleased, to send us his hand print each year.'

O, a tracing of his hand

'Just flat it out on a piece of paper and trace round it and send it to us. We can tell how he coming from that: even see if he be of *conversion stock* or strong and self-willed.'

They says they just lay it
in they palm, fer holding and puts
they hand on it, fer touching

Well, they be his 'promised parents' they done even not put a legal name to him. We practiced all the time trying to says it. *Manongi,* it be in the middle tween his grandpa's names: 'Tyrone Manongi Brown! ' And each year come'd six, they puts – from the first they done it – puts his hand on the paper; like this his parents done *show'd* and goes to tracing bout it. I tells Tyrone, that be *indian talk* he be speaking to them that gifted him of his middle name and that be why he put his hand on paper fer tracing. Touching, aint it?

O me and Tyrone wanted to see that parade. Snow Festival Day it were. It really be me done wanted to see that parade but I put the light in Tyrone's mind. I wouldnt be lone if I be with somebody. So we planned past my Aunt Lil's intentions, cause she aint never allow me to go to no town *Lone.* She says: *'the town be far way over the hills,'* of which we seen only one – as we be little – the one filling in the sky of the backyard. The firm-fright hymn in her voice: *'...and I dont want you over near the basin waters...'* put *me gainst the wall,* most times but always with my imaginations of the parade.

WE done must wrap over wrap cloth the foot well afore placing on the shoes and take the lamp of oil light, being the journer need step all day into the night to return. And in our plan we gots to take count of one place of our tracks cause we most might forgit the way in all that excitement of the parade and such. We'd beg of a apple from Miss Ink Pen, the poem lady up the road – who puts everything people'd do in her Sunday poems fer church. We'd needs a shelter to stop-in, long the way. A great card board box s'do.

O Tyrone, we gots
to practice the it

Fer weeks me and Tyrone, sit fixed in church on sundays praying fer help fer our trip. One sunday the answer come'd in the afternoon. We followed closely and thought on the foot tracks laid by Reverend Papa Dyke's tale-at-testifying bout Sister Ruths' faithfulness on her *trips* to town. He'd raise his hands looking to the 'Wheres' and call in *divine language:* 'Hear me, Lord, I sometimes thinks on her leanings-towards-home-form, interrupted occasionally when a curlicueing kind of wind'd be caught up and under puffed out and ballooned her over garment. She'd gather it all in light her old oil lamp...O, I most remembers amber glo's on the snow! She be a most faithful woman. She would gather all our wants from the town cause in the middle of the week, hardly none of our women folks could go to town so she done it fer the whole community. Usually on a Thursday.

'She'd pack a small kerchief of fruits and dates, Lord, put on her *"age"* — a coat of many tales and lots more years of wear in it. Wrap wool around her tired neck and hands; be sure to carry her old lamp of oil light from the railroad and some of the big "Red Ball" matches. Wednesday nights, most of our folks met at the church fer singing and uplifting. That's when we give her our wants. Spices and such. Nothing too much to carry and messages of rememberances to the town folks; letters of specialness fer to post; prayers fer keeping safe and we'd leave a good stoked up fire in the church stove fer her in the morning to git warm'd by. Great God!

'Early in the morning, Miss Ruths'd, O she'd get out some early; before the *before of us* even not been risen, and mostly we knowd she'd be gone cause of the tracks hers and the dogs here and about. But dont you know, the dogs got some such respect cause to my remem-berancings, they aint never barked awake anyone ever when Miss

Ruths, be up round and on her way. AMEN! But just let anyone else come *anyone else come* day or night especially night *specially night* them hounds is some loudness.

'Miss Ruths'd first go to the church to warm up and pray. Then she'd set out up on her journey. *All* morning she'd walk to town and she says her dress would drag and freeze at the hem some days cause of her ankle sweat and due to the meltings and freezings that be occurred along the way small puddles and such.

'You know, just before the basin there be a small valley like place which always is filled with warm air no matter what the weather be around it. O folks often'd talked in some whispers with they heads low-bowed when they speaks about the "whys" of that hot place. Miss Ruths, says she stopped there many times, cleared snow from the rocks to rest her belongings on and knelt down to pray; thankful fer the steps she'd been allowed to made and asking fer to continue. She'd always pass some words in the warm valley

She were a most faithful woman

'Then she'd walk to – cross the FROZEN basin

'When she were done in town it be dark again and she'd start the journey back. AMEN. Now we all knowd she'd be coming back so we'd wait-watch fer her to come and as 'time be steady, yes, a first amber glint be motioning itselfs on the farthus hill sight – 8 o'clock, fer sure EVERYTIME HARELDING! and our folks was please to "Praise God! " and pass: "Here her a coming."

'Now that'd stir a shudder in you in them days; umh!

'Lord! her movement be heavy you see'd it in the way the glint be a moved and the lamp be hung a bit lower than is other wise. She carrying some packages. The lamp be assured to go out most likely, many times cause of the wind-nights. Miss Ruths'd, hide the lantern under her coat to protect the flame but every so often you'd hear a suck of air comed at the windows of our homes, where we be looking out following her comings, fer sure her light be blowed out and everything would stop. Even the wind seemed to hold up – give her time then of a sudden, a slight glint to amber magic'd up and its half hidden movements to: "She be pressing on..." shouts and laughins: "Lord, that woman." Such 'd please us. As she neared home we'd all go out to meet her and help her to the church. The memory staggers but fer years I waited fer that glo on the snow topped hills and that woman Miss Ruths, leaning, come farward in our ways that lantern light making zig zags of sways and such...'

It be with these thoughts on the travelings of Miss Ruths, that me and Tyrone come'd to start our trip to the town and to the parade – when we come'd tired we stop, sit in our shelter-box, eat on our apple and sings:

be a sprinkle on a pickle;
be some fuzzy milk or pimples
on a wrinkle
be a hickey on my heart
be the last part of a froart
be a squat
be a squach...

The basin be frozen so we could walk on it. We heard the musics and come'd up on the crowd.

Peoples marched in the road too a clown who stood hind of his face (what he carried on a stick and we followed it into the up's and down's he played at the crowd) laughed hollows and echos at us. There be fat folks in jolly dress *bean poll man* come'd and MISS TATTOO TIT WOMAN advertizements on the sides of the dairy wagon caught our gaze. Then come'd the mayor and the parade queen and princesses; majorettes, a pipe band with fife, fire wagon with fine horses to pull a gap in the parade and what come'd be white folks dressed in black leotards, grass skirts, with coal dust on they faces and strange black cotton wire hair – screaming, hollering and staggering up and down on a flat bed wagon, O, me and Tyrone, wants to see everything wants to walk long with the music wagon what puffed smoke and funny music ...and we done. The side walks be some moving the crowd push-swayed and peoples slip'd-fell'd all round us in sounds of joyousness and I thought on the church: 'What if the Lord, come'd now and caught us? ' The parade were in a happiness done scared to fright in me. All round us be this *sound* and the buildings come'd kept'd live over us in echos.

We brung our shelter me in front and Tyrone in back. One time I carried it walking backwards but that aint work none...cause I slip'd and the crate box fell, hitting this big lady on the ankle. She yelled and stomped a bend in our shelter all in the same motion.

Some horses come'd pass and one fell down cause of stepping in the poop-mess of horses gone afore. A holler went-gone from the crowd to a great puff cloud of breaths it be:

'SHIT, LADY! '

Pout lip, bad mouth Tyrone done done it. It werent no squeak of softness but a high to scale tone baby-voice-shit-lady! Seem'd the whole parade turned and look on us as awfulness, the whole of awfulness's in the world. The big lady be facing me and when Tyrone done spoke she turned hopping...hitting him in the face with her hip side and knocking him down "square". The woman stomp'd agin on our box and with a twisted-chopped-mouth-almighty, she come'd loud: 'GOD STRIKES WITH A QUICK AND MERCILESS VENGEANCE, LITTLE BOY.'

I seen her ankles – come'd red – in black salt-sweaty shoes as she walked pass whilst I bent to help Tyrone stand up. More crowd come'd round us who aint knowd what happened so we pulled-straight our shelter picked up and moved on monst them. A wornout pipe band were hardly to be heard. To tell the truth, I aint heard much of nothing else the rest of the walk. The new crowd we be in, be the end of the parade and a push come'd a fuss bout us. Me and Tyrone, be all eyes of fear cause some-most look-a-look to us like we be the same from them on the wagon: the white play niggers drunk and jump-staggering on they flat bed wagon; the crowd screaming and yelling with them at us.

We come'd to the park by the sea and the cold made its presents knowd again. People disappeared while me and Tyrone be rubbing our eyes of tired and sting. The snow hadnt melted none much in the park. Tyrone say his ears be cold and started crying. I put our shelter on its side and we crawled in close together:

'We'll rest then go home.'

'Which way that be...'

Tyrone say in tear talk...

'Besides, I be hungry and my jaw got a hole in it from where that fat woman knocked me down.'

He tried to show me and spit some red out the shelter on the snow. It warmed up a bit to fog Tyrone *tuned up* some tears and cried up to sleep.

They say that on some cold nights the sea fog be alive
and so strong that it can snatch you soul way just as
you open out to breath.

I wakes to wood burning smell my Aunt Lil's silence; my sister Charles-etta over in the corner peering out through the window-sweat and Uncle Nough holding his face in his work gloved hands. I coughed but didnt recognized me in it. Aunt Lil burst: 'O MY BABY PRECIOUS...' into tears and grab hold'd me with a protection I've done since hoped and prayed the 'Wheres' might belove me with; cepting I aint never want the fear that come'd later in Aunt Lil's touch as she be holden me. I bit down hard on my jaws and determined (stubborn'd) no tears cause her hug were so that it hurt-crunch me. Were then I thought on this: 'Where is Tyrone? ' I kind of jerk as some of Aunt Lil's tears fall on my neck and runs a bit to my back. Never let go my jaws I knowd, with no more thinking God, do be merciful

We is pleased to think on him curled
up like a fuzzy walker worm

Tyrone, you put coal dust on the snow man's face trying to make it real. Little boy, you aught not been with such fuss with veins popping out all over from what's a inner center of rage.

somedays I looks for a thought of you and done be a thing there even darkness from behind my eyelids dont bring them spot-images of somethings that sometimes gets me started so I haves to just lay back and scratch in my head next of my ears which sets interest in a different itch: thinking of you.

if I could have saved the dryness from my tears by now a salt mound be in the palm of my hand O, proof's locked up in the silence of the walls.

Strutter'd pass gas on his knees praying to get through *'doing down here'* and go in the somewhens of where *'trouble'* will be at rest. He thought on Tyrone's funeral; gazed through til his thoughts burst open on a emanation surrounded by spirit and beauty: Aunt Lil, of wrinkled winks, crinkled old smiles and percimmony lips of shy. That woman sho could go fer religion.

O, CEASE FROM

She'd sing out: 'Yesss...' *sustain it!* while pushing way the 'wheres' — they didnt have no thing to do with her — Lord! It means: her hand went right up fore her face; palm-flat-out holding back! and let towards her 'Yesss': just a linger-to-silence.

NE-VER
grow old On High
Meet with your friends
your mama;
your papa...
me soul-glad!

Then she'd lay back to herselfs and mosquito-hum, hoarse FLARES, strained next of a 'oooh! ' crunched up to a smile buried in her chins she'd pinch the center-ruff, come'd tween her eyebrows:

'I best believes
most of all, you'll meet
The Glory Man
O! it take some courage
Sure-Really'

She'd stood wide-leg to sturdy herselfs rock-stretched her arms, hands-reached til her whole selfs come'd a asterisk!   that some special character, shaped like a star. A real force of spirit come on to Strutter. He'd been staring at a *lamp,* closed his eyes in light and seen some shadows of dust swimming round under his lids. A slightness of chill brung him to Aunt Lil's singing: *'Arborescent* in the middle of the *forest frondescence'* (so says, Reverend Dyke). She served in the choir of Daughter Ruth's with the Reverend Papa Dyke, interrupting talking the attention to himselfs. They done this in three-quarter-time-goodness; sang; through shouts, cryings, tamborines and clappings: (ALL)

'God, *(sustain it!)*...will/ be watch-ful-of yoouuu...! ' SANG it!

Aunt Lil'd come from some right-weighty depths   crescendo'd quiet as to flow over the herd of sound: 'I want to talk about Him' Daughter Ruth, shouted through her tears

repeat it!
repeat it! yaw

all done it:

'God,

(the altos pushed out the harmony to *lift* and turned up the)...will/'

cut it clear

Aunt Lil's solo ascending, one note left'd hanging/   'Wahaaahum' answered, turned, a over high squirl'd-skinny-pressed-air hum: 'ooooh, beneath His wings   ...He will be watchful of you' – the choir trailed- '...watch-ful-of-you.'

'Let me sit. Rest awhile! ' The Reverend shouted as he walked round, wipen a 'why' AND some sweat way. Aunt Lil, pump'd: 'The Lord!   the Lord!   the Lord, whispers...' and with sudden forte '/YESSSSSS,' – the choir – 'oooooooouo! /au-oooh'd,' Reverend Dyke, FLARED-in-hoarse, up to a scream'd loud: 'SAAAACRED   SE-CRET...' His head drop'd as he went on speaking the rest, scrumbled in rhythm to Aunt Lil's obbligato'd: 'ooooooOOOOH, PREcious; in that great gitting up from now! '

Rev: 'Yes.' (with a soft tremolo)

STRUTTER, tween what fall on the floor, laments Tyrone's death:

When you gits so quiet like as to be able to hear the ticking of a watch on the wrist whilst it be in your pocket: then you gonna know the deepness of from where my screams comes and why folks dont hear them, cause them *screams* have so far-to-coming that the sound goes soft at the roof of my mouth to a 'mmp! '

I thinks I be a good person. Least I tries to treat every people right. But I live in a evil world; my mirrors be dirty; the mirrors round me be dirty and I caint see to know *too* well so I dont *knows* fer sure if I be good. I thinks on it tho, and these days I be pretty sure, to much, that in my own mind, where I be left'd to myselfs most, I aint all that bad.

3. Strutter's Grandmother

I were in the feeling of grandma when she were learnt how to write-make, fer the first time, the numbers 8 and 6; her age at the moment. O she just want to drawing *her* 8 and 6 together, all over the anywhere's. Walls, ice box, and the likes. Big shaky 8's and little loopidy 6's one larger than the other. She even played round with the design of it, filling the insides up: 'A full 86 I be' ...bent over and done school girl drawed it in the floor squared it and danced bout it, hop scotch like.

She'd stand back, close her face in humble ways shake her head press her hands to her breast and pump breath: 'Lord, praise; look at them numbers, I be! ' Grandma aint care-worry bout there being more numbers one's, two's, five's and such like: 'Hush, child. I aint gonna ask the Lord, fer *more* numbers. I might caught to learning who then gonna call me wise again? '

She just proud as goodness to make, so she can see, *her* 8 and 6. They never be on a straight line that schooling done showed and sometimes the 6 done laid down someone'd say: 'Look it, grandma, the 6 done laid over' and grandma's *stomp* it were: 'LEAVE IT! It done matter none cause they is mines. Aint it? ' She even passed it on to Uncle Fish, but he come'd to learnt a pyramid crossed above its right point and a 6. He worked at a paper factory and sometimes were known to hide out in there when he were tired and didnt feel like working. But he'd always get caught after he learnt 4 and 6 cause he were so fasten-taken-up with them numbers that he'd practice a trail of them on the skids of paper right to where he be rest-hiding. He even not put 4 and 6 on his pay checks in the place of where his name is to be written. PROUD, believe it!

My room: I been meaning to tell bout it afore but it changes. Hell, I be in the same place all the time but fer days at will, the room could become'd who ever I remembers or what ever I thinks on. The walls be painted white, you knows, the kind that covers any-everything though, there's some 'flowers-by-a-bird' wall paper come up through in spots and some fly and mosquito swats be there where I done killed them all over the place. I near always keeps the draw curtains closed bout the windows. Sometimes the sun done come'd through and make a garden in which mine and other shadows *loose'd shape and appear,* changing walls. That's nice, aint it. Sometimes I sit in the middle of the wind. And sometimes it be all black cause my hands covers my tears...If I steps, a certain creak in the floor will tell where I be and others, where I been. O yes: and water drip on the green growing in my sink.

4. Oak Tree

More than else, Miss Queeny, looked close to much, like a skinny black clothed bird. Bobben. She'd be bent firm toward the ground hoeing at her vegetable rows in back of her place.

O she were a wonder in that!

She'd hoe a bit   drag herself to the next hoeing spot, while also, slopping along a bucket filled with water and a dipper spoon, which she'd drink from or pass over the back of her neck...as she felt pleased to do.

The humming she'd do
ore my soul! the wind would
swoop-swach take up her tune thought
among the neighbor children who'd
propose 'they' words:

'Pick the sun and burn your fingers...' as they played *wagon wheel,* a kind of movement in a circle with no hub – they'd stretch an arm out and touch fingers, one finger stretchen from a fist to the middle and if you lose touch: '...fox fleas play on the square of your apron.'

Her dust faded-to-the-ground dress, – a grey checked table cloth apron layed in the lap place over it – would clear in tween the rolls behind her in that the hem of her dress would catch-gather loose soil and drag cover the where-ever she beens, in neat furrows...that is all cept the square holes made by her old nuns' shoes   the heels sunk too deep to erase.

Birds were known to fly dive
at her as she be working and
she'd: 'git! ' some mingled humming
and angry sounds...but not long

Most folks come'd to believe that a ghost walked among her garden. They say: over the years, someone is always to see this white-glowy-silk-sheeted thing dancing circles round the garden about the fourteenth night from the showing of the *moon of spring.* But my granddaddy told the right of it. He say that: 'Old Miss Queeny were like a fox. She study the wolves and on that certain presence – that be the "*moon of spring*" – after sunset, she'd drink two, maybe three, hot pots of tea right down at once! Then in the night she'd circle her garden *PEEING!* to mark place, that the opossum, porcupine and the deer might respec and know not to enter mong her tomatoes vines and corn stalks.'

O elegant this dance of wet waste which the madam
done. She'd pinch pick up the hem of her pink pale
nighty - little peaks they were; went right with her –
flow-flopping. Danced in bucks and bows. Done it
in squats and tip toe runs in tween tears of
spring-moon light; DONE IT IN SILENCE!
Yet her whole form be presenting the slightest shut-
ter of: WHEE!

That done it right! The woman had the *Example* when it come'd to gardening. And she werent taken to greed but shared with *all;* even to passing, over her fence, the soft ripe and worm touched vegetables, a show of appreciating to the animals she'd locked out in the spring.

When winter come'd, the old folks'sd watch everybodies chimney and as they'd see no smoke from Miss Queeny's place they'd send a boy running to bring her a thatchet of wood, some bread, snuff and a gallon jug of coal oil. Then he'd ask if there'd be anything she'd wish from the store.

Grand-daddy say: 'My grandmother seen no smoke in Miss Queeny's stack and called me to run the erron. She say she aint see'd Miss Queeny for two days and aint noticed no steam wet on her windows neither. "So you go to the store, son. Bring that old Queeny what be on this list...and put the question for what she be of need when you delivers it." '

He went on: 'Us childrens talked many funny thoughts of that woman and we-all fear, most assuredly, the wind path that blow from her place, spit her vegetables out when served at our table — at the knowings we gonna git beat — even dogs is said to pass her door with they heads bow'd low and they tails tween they legs! So you can see I aint want to do this erron running. But grand-mother had a long hard wood cane and no reserve to use it. She believed in respec and taught it to me from back of my neck. I did this thing but waited two hours back hind the store before I delivered the stuff.

'As I come'd to Miss Queeny's door, I dreamed a lot and when I knocked I waked-jerked myself up from the fear thoughts I had of her. Miss Queeny opened the door and *loved me to come in* but I pressed the things to her without looking up. Fastly I turned, started to leave but she say: "Hey. Wait child."

'I come'd round to meet her face. She'd been crying. Us childrens say her *crying* were so long that spring wiggles had time to grow within her tears.

'She say: "Wait," and took a nickel from a little home rag purse. O *Lord, I seen her hands:* "I caint, aint spose to take no thing for nothing." Then I remembered to ask her if she want anything from the store. She didnt hear me cause she be turning away: "Waaaait," she sound a echo then reached hind the door and *magic'd up* me a apple – quick as she do! "you take this but dont eat it fore you dinner. You hear? "

'I held the thing in the same outreach position I have received it – just about to see the poison in it – feel it sweat into the palm of my hand. Started off carrying it home that way. "Thank you, Mam." She didnt speak. I remembers her skirt dragging pass over her threshold the door closing. "Yes, you welcome" ...I told myself and, "go on home."

'I couldn't even give that apple away so I buried it a top the hill by the sea. Apples were hard to have in them days and I did feel some guilts. But I rubs my knee at the truth of my *fears.* O Miss Queeny, my proof be on the hill! I planted a apple but look there now – a old bent knotted-Queeny crooked, oak tree grew there! '

O I dreams of the roots
of that oak tree even
at this old age I be

5. Banished

I took to sucking eggs when I were six year. Just punch a hole in one one day and got caught to it. Well, fer years my people and the neighbor folks be interested in wondering what be sucking them eggs. Some say it were the dogs and on that thought, I laid convincing evidence. So fer years they'd chase the dogs off our place but as I continued to suck them eggs and times come to fall hard on our area, the folks took to shooting the dogs three of them it were before they done caught me sucking them eggs of my Aunt BeEtta's bantam hens and took forced tied me to the great oak tree on the River People's property fer me to wait the evil spirit of Mr. Monrove, the backslider, to come and take me to triune depths of darkness! Fer in them times, we wondered at the mind. O yes.

Often we thought on it it's comings: in the childrens; it's goings: in the old folks; and in tween: it left some with a secret! *Dumb to us all*...or with the giggles and the *dance* of no rhythm. And in our understandings, we was taught: *Fear Believe!* in the mind imaginings. Cause to be caught *up* in them were to be punished.

Fer a while I stood spread-legged balanced on the great roots, but my senses come'd scattered and I slunk tween them. Tis truth, fer I seen Mr. Monrove, coming out my shoe toes and from up underwards next of the roots: from hind my closed eyes, in tween everything and taste of his dead spirit from my tears...bitter on dry saliva spit.

O I do dreams yet awhile
of the roots

But I got a head on me Sho nough, go way Lord! Got a *head* on me. I took the thought: I too might grow there, tied as I were. I'd reverse the whole damn triune depth's thing to *heaven bound!*   Yeeessss, I too might grow there!   All night I were growing upwards as the tree ...It's that thought saved me from the worms.

You can guess the trouble my mind been in ever since. I were 14 year and that time they run'd *Me* off our place. I stayed in the world fer some years.

After I got chased from our home place, I went to town to live and as I grow'd young   I grab'd up me a horn. A old piece of horn, I played it   some-later; but I done it; loud!   with feelings and hummed the notes I couldnt as yet make so that the rhythm would be continued. I learn real fast. Fer years I pulled the *coat tail* of Sleepy, the guitar man; Lame Jack, the fastest fingers on the keys; Iron Chops, the sax man and Mr. Monday, who played with black drum sticks, to teach me how and all they knowd bout music. I practiced at all hours   in the barns and garages of my buddies in town. I, I slept with it   the only real love I knowd fer a long time. I'd rather practice that horn – beat up as it were – than go play *'run in the dark'* with my friend-girl, which I always talked into hiding out – most cause running werent not what I had a mind to do. She never mind. But when that horn come'd, I were possessed of it and lost that girl.

They says that *Bow-legged* Timmons, got that way by blowing too hard. So I done just the right thing. I always blow'd leaning up gainst a wall fer support; and when I first played my 'leaning' way in the 'UP N' DOWN' club, it were so cool the peoples just scream'd with hollerings. Tho...

I guess I just remembers a pain there too.

I done once, read in crescendo a book   O I gots carried by the phrase
to the top of my voice and at the end of my reading there be lots
of clapping from outside my door. Now that dont qualify me as no
preacher but if I had my means of it...

My ceiling be a crack split right from end to end of my room. The
plaster done swelled at the center, left the framing structure and
there's other little swollen's that I talks to when I walks under them.
I'm always moving my cot.

And I writes notes to myselfs like: I loves you all too well; please
wake up safely...   and I puts it by my head so it be the first thing
I sees when I opens my eyes.

When you looks into the air and begins to talk to yourselfs and the
surrounds, you hears and participates; the corners comes *live*   the
pictures on the hanging places be patient with you and the lamp
light and the motion that your heart keeps you in, all comes *one.*

I try to remembers to open the window when I wakes cause it do get
smelly in the night from me sleeping with my mouth a gap.

Part II

Leaving Home

'that lonesome spot
will come in on you'

I. Ruby Jean

O, Ruby Jean
you be the wonder
the 'WHERES' is neither
whispered·bout

Elision (To be read in tempo)

Ruby Jean

Her hands drew much attention point pecking slicing comma accenting rhythms and they sang out in snaps. At times they played in delicate semi-circles or hung limp:

my man done...
damn-you-my-man!

Her fingers extended everywhere and come back to hold they own palms. She put her forehead to her fist and mumble sanging:

Don't try to tell me he loves me
not when you see me crying like this
my greatest enemy's my own imagination
and time
to think...

A woman's voice broke the smoke in the bar room yes'd her on in whispers: YES! YES! YES! and Texas Red's saxaphone scream'd hearty scraping air tones in response to that woman and life her whispers to ringing shouts from the crowd:

YESSSSS!
(Yes. Tell it!)
Ruby Jean!
Ruby Jean!

Don't you know, the blues make everyone's body feel tube-hollow and wiggly it be pushing up what's in you and agitating you on to cry out

Ruby Jean took a lit cigarette handed her to from out of the darkness stuck it in a corner place of her lips. Smoke rolled up her face had her squinting one eye. Her head lifted and light cast from ceiling beams done touched high cheeks and her sweaty brow. Mr. Jess Arthur's organ eased in, from somewhere, in its upper register a mood of sweet mercifulness sustained over a deep low rumbling bass. Ruby Jean had it to sang but it weren't coming. Teeth marks creased her lips and her left hand thumb were trying to scratch off its index finger. Her arms spread-rise floating put to the breeze of sound from the horn's moaning... and gesture, COME.

Come hold me, Lord

Her head dropped; trying to shake out the words but no sound. She stood there a skinny thin frame then with the slightest of flitter jerk, again she tried to get it out. Screams come up to her throat but be stopped by her closed eyes, clinched teeth; the sound gutteral and choked ...and her mouth such a bitter shape! She closed her elbos in on herself and rocking doubled over this push forced up a

Please!   send me someone to warm my feet at night
Ain't I got a right to ask

...and it were holy.

Every word she sung dug deep in and come'd up full from inner places filled with need and guilt. A man (on the run so to speak) cried out: 'Come on to my house, baby, I warm more then your feet. For free! ' She lent him no mind. And flat laughing noises, his too heavy to ride the smoke would fall; an embarrassment. In the time it takes Ruby Jean to catch her breath, Texas Red's sax discribed the scene by making a pointed *funky* adlib version of the first four bars of *'DIRTY OLD MAN GO WASH YOUR MOUTH OUT BLUES! '* Mr. Jess Arthur's organ roared in with fart-grunts and quicked the tempo completed by a loud lowest 'E' from the bass a sign of most disapproval aimed in the gentilman's direction. Uh muh. All agreed.
Ruby Jean turned it go now; every bit...and led the crowd with each note to her judgement:

When you see the clouds coming
and caint hear the birds singing
please don't track my kitchen floor

Don't bring yourself home
done swept way your footprints
from out front my door

Oscar Jackson, the pimp, burst visible cryings and let meaning to the woman's song. A mumble of explanation sprang up.

We met one night when she be put to weep and moaning by some of the men in the club. I dont meddle I learnt not never to do this very early when I come'd to the club. But this woman's tears entered your inners and caused your detached-selfs to forms a spot fer curiousity to come and stir up yourselfs. Well, you knows, you be moved and gots to ask, so I done: 'Miss Ruby Jean, is you of need? ' She aint answer but seemed to quiet a bit which told me to ask agin. Done. I dont remembers how but I asked her to: 'Come go to my house.' Done. She be there some time and spoke of food. Course, I be in care of somebody and I aint have much. She cepted a bowl of soup and dont you knows, that woman is warm! So warm. It's in her smile.

In time ever, we went on to her place. She kept company with another man who visited in all places and were sometimes, to most, not around but I be mindful of this, so'd I had to leave her at they door.

And Strutter'd wake from this thought mad at some...he'd cover up with a shout-out: 'LIFE IS SOME-COMICAL, aint it? It speak the truth! '

In the later, one of other mornings, I seen her fer breakfast...

O, it come'd to me

She were lumps and bulges in her morning gown, the lace bout her neck let you see through to what's left'd. One cup of tea be the usual: sometimes, toast. And near always, were the cutting up some old bread left'd over or purchased.

'I left'd to go way the day last week and members I aint feed a bird.
A tear come'd to me eyes Dear! how silly – '

Her words fall-drive down hill as she look to the 'wheres'.

'But I must be *let,* to forgits. You thinks?

'There's some meaning in it – I tell ya. So many years now. I feeds them and then curses them, when they dirts on me washing hanging out there. Lord! Mrs. Hooks, says to me, in the voice of many gum squeaks, she says,'

(and her voice let to tell it in image her tongue wash-stretching mongst her gums – thus the splash of squeaks):

'Ruby Jean you aught not to feed them birds in the summer time. You aught just feed them in the winter. That way they dont dirt on our cloths when they's hanging out.

'But I feeds them anyways I aught; and I does. Well, I gots to...' and trailing off – her hand squeeze her eye brows together, then fall over her nose to catch a yawn and end pinch a night-slobber tween her fingers

(O, sweet woman
you must of been)

'So many years now. Hell, they's lots of soap but they aint plenty of birds no more. Is they.'

It werent no question. She says all them sayings during the thinking on the wrinkles bout her eyes. She done. Her fingers pressing them wrinkles stretch and the sleep way – a fore it were...

Listen. This be Aaron, Lord:

I been talking to myselfs in whispers pulling my chin to a point and sitting real still ceptin, there be more aggitation in my shadow than I cares to let on with. So I turns off the light. Some dust come'd, make a horizon on the darkness and let a vision afore me: open up on bare feets walking on dirt wet bricks to the market place. Every four in the a.m. she goes there. Ruby Jean, shoes tucked under her arms and laughins. It's onion soup she gits there, coming home in her shiny green dress on the rust red of blue dust here round my room.

The suck on my gums gives her a voice, pitiful: mouthings of soundlessnesses in spit, afore long come'd moans in *whatever thoughts* I lays; overlays: 'Woman, what you come'd to? defines so much in me.' and repeats; til she laughs at me. Her hair'd stand swept'd up over herselfs, rolled a top her head in lost ways, some comb'd and come'd fergot around her face ... be something to remind you... and she laughs at me – gives me the thumb, but says she dont takes no credit! and walks into a disappear: humming hymns in the high mosquito tones; then she'd quiet. Cause

'that lonesome spot
will come in on you'

the rest be spilt in the floor tween my feet.

Lord be overshadowed and like a broken disc. I am caught on the gaze of rememberings and thoughts that stumble me, still me from my purpose.

2. War I.

I wept'd blurs; the cold and snot slowly dripping tween my feet to on the bare board. I aint no broken man. I been searching fer some rage in me: everyone ask bout it. It frown-up in me: 'How come all these things happen and you aint got no *rage* in you' that's what they asks... yet, it come's more and more something suggested: signs and symbols; or played out afore my eyes; even not *set up,* then legislated to envolve me...pull me on in my mind not knowing the real truth of it and I be squirming, standing on the edge of a highest cliff afraid to follow my own echos on out over the *else.*

Strutter'd pear off, begin to talk to a flocking of gull-birds he imagined mocked him from the *'Wheres'.* I ask: Why come I gots to accept that there aint be no God, cause the *ruling* systems dont work no more? His eyes went bleary. He rubbed his fist past them like he were boxing, then pressed them closed, his fingers pulling towards the center bove his nose to pinch the half drying wet what's left: Me, Tedum and Big Casters be on this ship going over in the War I, when we be stopped at this shore in France cause they were bombing and shooting the place and we couldnt go no ferther so we be landed. It were Mother's Day and Tedum: well, we all be scared of fright but Tedum be crying fer his mama. In the craft you dont see nothing. you just hears the war and Tedum's were bove the chaplain's prayer. I means I tried to keep him cool: 'Tedum, as soon as we lands, man, I wants to talk to you' but that aint done no good. Big Casters, just stood, tree-like looking at the sky and smoke, as he werent not there.

We aint had no guns cause we be mess personnel. I were thinking on that when somebody signaled the sign, the craft hit the shore and we hauled ass out into – O MY GOD! Tedum, run'd off screaming, MAMA then looked snatched into the ground. I see'd it and claw's at my chest thought I done had a stroke but Big Casters, grab'd-pushed me into a trench and I come'd round quick. The only sound I can remembers be that of a baby crying, being rude-waken'd hard when my daddy haves a fight with my mama: 'MAMA! ' the hollar burst and I laugh'd-grab'd: 'BIG CASTERS, IT'S TEDUM! God Damnit! Tedum. Where you? '

'Oooooo, Mama. Maaamaaaaaaaaaaaa! O Lord.

'I'm in the *SHIT HOLE,* Aaron.'

AND IN THE MIDDLE OF THE ENTIRE WAR THERE WERE A SILENCE.

Then laughins. From in the trenches, my whole platoon started up and come'd to laughins. War I, all around us and we laughins! ... that is all cept two. Big Casters, stood bent in breathless whimpers, on one elbow leaning in up gainst the trench wall like he were pissing but baring his teeth, his eyes clamped on sweat and Sargent Strongst, our white officer, laid open dead bout Big Casters' feet. My eyes glazed; mouth dried: 'MAN? ! ! '

The nightmare still be a test and I aught sure come'd to know'd my-selfs then...

Tedum stayed in the hole fer three days cause we be pinned down fer that long til the support showed up. We had to crane him out of there and chisel him down but the smell aint washed off fer some time.

There be times during the war, a prisoner could ask to be your valet and one come'd to take a liking to Big Casters: the special prisoner of Big Casters. O, he were so nice. He were the enemy but somehow he were a nice man. He got the the laundry. He, he made the food. He cleaned anything he would; and with a smile, too, fer Big Casters. One day, Big Casters, says: 'Well, I'm tired of im. I guess I'm gon have ta kill im.' I stared at the ground. Then look at Big Casters and wonder: What kind of oppress...what kind of feeling this man done had all of his life that now he should kill anything that resemble him of the past and I try to plead but he says: 'You wont know nothing bout it til I decide.' I thought on the face of the smiling enemy, who soon gonna die and I walked way.

Sho nough, one day we out on the warf and long come the man bringing Big Casters his laundry. Big Casters, was holding a rifle now. The man come'd Big Casters, talk fast, pointing it like a command; some spit come'd with the loss of pitch in his voice near the end: 'Put the laundry down.

'Look out ta sea.

'Go ta the edge.

'Look out ta sea, see there's a pretty sight! '

The man become'd a question mark then tried to look interested and sort of like a child do, stepping farward in new shoes, he purpose-planted his feet in toward the direction but Big Casters, shout:

'NAW! NAW! Come on back here,

'Put-the-laundry down.'

He done.

His skull bone pressing on the flesh that unanswered – what? – the enemy just walk to the end of the warf – like he know'd something – and looked out to sea.

Big Casters, shot him and he fell in.

The gull-bird:
Screams, of red-rust-brown,
spilled, ground'd in mire
and smoke smug

... It's sanctified.

Big Casters, stayed over seas after things be over; says he aint never gonna come back to north america. But I dont know.

Strutter'd shout from his thoughts: '...and TIME! Ask me that? When no body wants you in they *time* and all the rhythms in your life are counting the times time til the *"over there"* ah *"after while"* or *"beyond Jordon"* and shit is to be. YES! THAT GREAT COLLECTION IN THE 'WHERES! ' You be grow'd up in that and left counting everything *less* than itselfs to lesson the wait and singing always humming: "It wont be long til we leave here fer that SOMEplace..." Why the hell they asking me fer the *time* and *place* huh? I already WAS-THEN-AM. Aint nobody wrote it down? – and come'd now, I just see'd fer to ask *why,* cause I dont know why, I... You best better bet, I-do-*be,* tho; and I'm telling you the *time* and *place* of it be under your fingernails; persistent! when you scratches your head in wonderment trying to give *me* place. Persistent, even not if you cuts the hell out of them nails short! ' Strutter'd look way from his old mirror and mumble himselfs across the room to his knees fer prayer. 'O Lord... – he'd jump from a sound and takes his prayer from it. O Lord, there's a point when I be aware of my tears drop falling on the leaf of a page in my phone book – you know, I'm always in my phone book, open to a blank page but not quite turned so it hangs in limbo-ways. You know, the page is bout to turn but wont more drops try to... no they just falls and fer sure now the page will only bounce a pretense to push up the wet. It's the tap sound I'm trying to tell you bout. The tear tap sound noise, that's what my cryings be like. O Lord, when will you find me I be truly alone.'

3. L.A.

It's with the old notes we haves to carry through

Hope! Strutter snap-jerk his head up as though somebody done says it out loud to him; cept it be inside his own head that the word come'd 'Hope' what the hell's... he motioned himselfs trying to shake it off; mumbled no's and yes's to his thoughts til he come'd to a beginning: 'O the longest trip I ever made (cepten the war) were in January one year. It were with the boys out to California. Snooks, the trumpet man, and my friend (my home boy) had wrote me to come and play music out to L.A. and bring him a drummer: That Bennie fellow is the one I wants. He wrote me to come soon as could. I needed that news cause my music were gone beyond the people here and they'd come'd to laughins at my playing so different. But *jazz* done touched the spirit in me and...well, Snooks done blessed me and I rushed to Bennie's home. 'Bennie, man. Snooks wants you and me to come out to California to play music. Man, he done *made it* and aint fergot us. Some righteous! Aint it.'

There be Coolie, another drummer and Took, the alto sax man at Bennie's kitchen seated at the table and when I says bout the letter they both says: 'We gonna come too.' I told them that Snooks aint had but room fer two. Me and Bennie! But Coolie, says: 'Have some *shit,* man.' He offered me what we *used* then; pushed it across the table whole nutmeg and cola, it were; together that stuff'd make you two peoples all in the once. I chew'd and drank and come'd agin: 'Man, he aint got no room but fer us.' I looked at Bennie, who's head be down.

Coolie: 'Man, I gots aunts and uncles all over the damn place! I gots a place to stay.' (with one of them shit looks that says you aught know me...)

Took: 'Me too. I gots a aunt.'

Strutter: 'Took, you dont even know'd who your mama is. What you talking on a aunt bout and besides, let it beknownced that you gots to git there and that takes *money.'*

Took: 'Aw man, look. (he magic'd up a dollar and grinned yellowish) I gots me a dollar and all I needs to done is make me some sandwishes to last me till I gits to my aunt there, babies, yeah! ' (this afore he had a taste of *shit* in him yet)

Coolie: 'We going man. Took, can stay with me.' (he says it with *no face* so I couldnt react to but instead, think on it)

Took: 'SEE? Yeah.'

(mosquitoe like)

her voice be like over *high*
and in the breeze

fragil; as parade streamers
holding on to:

'Lord. (up) *Lord.* (higher) *Lord...'*
curling the sound round of tongue

and letting it go
swelled up in air;

and *disappearing,*
come'd a hound's bayin do...

the gull-birds called:
when she died, she dropped
sudden-still   like
a wild thing;
felled

Poor Bennie's mama. I just can call back her eyes: half-lid'd, purtruding rust   and her hand, always press-pushing her face in squints to the left   a aura of *whisht.* He werent neither righteous with her and fussed her mind in worryins. Lots. She work her life to save him   got him some drums; got him out of all troubles. I never seen her sun-soul'd-selfs come'd like old folks's spose'd to; no never and...well, this time he stole her car. Sure, it be a old car: 'Man, we got to go, aint we? Mama know me; she aint gonna mind.'   And we be on our way.

There were a loud and happy send off from the *Up and Down Bar* room. All our friends and other drunks   and we cleared the town dreaming of Snooks, his *beach house* (which he done spoke of in his letter) and his new open air car. California, what must it be like; it's womens, places to go, our music being played *out there;* O, the thoughts! Bennie's mama's car were got second hand from what the highway patrollers had so it could still run fast and Bennie, liked to drive just like that, even though the roads aint so good as now. The nutmeg and cola done done its work! Took, went to singing the music of his new hero, Mr. Lester: 'Babies, listen.' He'd put some dribblings on his lips and come'd with this lie-of-note sound: 'O (laughins) Mr. Lester! Is you telling us the *truth?'* Took, be right pitiful but Coolie, started to *thoom* out a bass line to Took's dribble noise and afore long we all were singing something that sounded *right!* Cept fer Bennie, have his foot on the FLOOR. *'MAN?'* and talking to the car as like it be human: 'GO! GO! GO! ' laughing; when Took, looked up from a *hot like lick* to see two head lights in our path coming right our w... 'GO! GO! ' ... A rub-ba-do-ba, Took, in time to his *lick:* 'LOOK OUT, BENNIE! A CAR COM...' the cola and nutmeg stalled the *ing.*

Bennie: 'TURRRRRRRRRNNNNNnnnn! '

We'd seen the moon rise three times that night and the sun were to rise-set and rise agin in the morning all in one hour. Bennie, never stopped his fast driving cept fer...

Coolie: 'Stop the car, man.'

Coolie, went to the side of the road then. Took, crossed his legs and sniffed the air. Always sniff the air. Still it come'd to six days: two by a lake and that be in Arizona hot and: 'STOP the car, Bennie, man. Took? I caint right stand this heat and your stink man. I gonna throw you in that lake and you gonna wash your dirty ass.' Took, done this to no words of protest and such like.

It be night and we done drove up on the ocean full og'd on nutmeg and cola, bout surprised, more than it takes to curl the dogs' tail, at the black sea trying to grab us from the highway and the inspired Took, composed right there his 'Symphony of Lips Sound to the Sea at Night in 4/4 time: Ba-loo-ba-bah-ba-blu-ba dee-blup! blup! '

Late we come'd to Los Angeles, LOST.

They says: 'What he mean to you, this friend? ' and I says: 'Huh, You wants it in words? What do the dream mean to the poor lone preacher "AFTER WHILE", mean to his shout a understanding answer mean to the thirst of his question? It mean hope, motivation and reward. When you lost, the voice of a friend can make you call on God's Name in thanks.'

'Aaron Strutter! you in town, man? ' Snooks's voice be sleepy but: Thank You, God. 'Yeah, man. We here on 52nd Palm House, in this place called Venice, under a street light. Is it fer When you coming? ' And when I come'd back to the car, *all* of me be in California. My heart be of notes clapping out the rhythm of YES: 'He coming right soon, cats.' Coolie, open his mouth to says something but...shit, we all be too glad. Instead we just jest in silence and together we done our *'all fer us-each'* hand shake and hugged in turn each other's eyes.

Werent long afore this old pink hump-back car smoked up to long sides of us and some talk come'd through the smoke like we being addressed by the genie which caused in me the jim-jams: 'Strutter, is that you, man? ' It be Snooks, and fer sure when the smoke cleared, I caint never conduct nobody to that place of joy I been in when I seen what

I could of him insides his car that night: 'Aw man, I'm so glad to see on you...' I gots from the car and past through the *genie-screen* into Snooks's car: 'Hi on ya.'

Snooks: 'Later man. I gots to git back quick cause I gots to work tomorrow so tell the cats, to follow me.'

I put my hand out the window like the general of some group and signaled to come after. Then I went on to talk on how Coolie and Took, come'd cause they gots to be there and that they gots a place to stay with Coolie's relations. And fer the next little while I be just silent. Thinking: *Where be Snooks's open air car?* We drove'd down the highway where the sea still grabbed at you with glo in its wave come-over like a warning and such like. Snooks seen me thinking on it and says it be the spirit of the moon riding on to the wave's back. Snooks done become'd poetical since he done moved here.

Then we come'd on some sand to another road and what scared me to shouts: 'Snooks, we in a oil field? '

Snooks: 'Well, man they is a few oil rigs bout here –'

We stopped to this yellow-street-light-lit-grey house and Snooks says that this be it. *His house on the beach! surrounded by the smells of gas and oil riggers...* I slow'd from the car right strange, the words of Snooks's letter filling my mind with questions but come'd I stepped through into the house my heart happied and I shouted: 'Home at last...' but right fast a echo come'd, *Home at last.* Somebody else living here? My question be hushed when the lights open'd up on a room near bare with one of them locker room grey benches. There be a gas stove heater with a little pan of rust on top of it and three curtainless windows – I were taken strange.

Snooks says: 'Welcome. That bench is fer Strutter to sleep on and the rest of you will haves to sleep on the floor. Be sure and put some water in that pan on the stove afore its lit and I aint gots no matches so if you gots some go ahead. I'm tired, cats, so see you later.' Snooks's words sort of sunk into the cola and nutmeg sleep on our faces and he disappeared into the bowels of the house and some squeakings told us he were in bed. Now I aint gonna be too stunned at all this cause the cola and nutmeg done done a job on me and since we be at *home,* the tension done left my body and I stretched straight on over the bench and fergot everything...

I come'd woke at some sounds: tappings at the window and callings on the name of Snooks. Coolie, started laughing wildly and Took, went into imitating the voice: *'Snooks, baby?'* Snooks, barefooted, passed us in the dark; tried to sound mad at the woman but rabbit-quick come'd pulling *the shadow of sweet smells* through the room: 'This here be, Feona Fureena, the dancer...cats.' Snooks were always polite no matter how come the why...Bennie, slept through it all – even the squeakings.

Coolie and Bennie suddenly come'd the best of buddys and they took the car off to Sacramento and sold it. Whither they done it or not, they says they took the money and went to San Francisco and had a big party. Anyways, when they come'd back they be broke and Coolie, informed Snooks, that he aint got no relatives in California anywheres and that he would have to stay on the beach. Took, it turned out have a aunt so we took him over there. She were alright fer a day but she aint like Took, gitting high on the stuff and she ask *the Lord!* to ask him to leave. Took, come'd home strange after that. I thinks that the nutmeg and cola be that period of time when it be the most important thing in our lives. We met all the people we wanted to meet but we always met them after we done used the stuff so everybody was wonderful. After the stuff, I never really know'd anybody that weren't not wonderful ceptin fer what my *friends* gonna teach me soon. Bennie, were the first to git a job. His drums be needed out there so he be the quickest to work. His name spread and we all come'd noticed out there. But them folks's slick. Musicians could just look at your music and have it in they mind and played it afore you could. My mouth be always open at they abilities bout stealing other folks's music. We went everywheres there be music. Sessions were all over the place the *main cats* on every horn and singers of all sorts, trying to out everything everybody. And womens trying to walk away with anybody and they always walk away with somebody. Everything else be a blur in my mind today cause the other else I seen were the highways. We spent all the rest of the time trying to git where we be going.

I have not to eat, so I aint, in days. I be gitting to weak and come'd so of a short time. Lord, it were the sickest day in my life. I spread out on the bench looking up at the yellow walls and in the *and* no time; no space. The phone spoken and I rolled off the bench and had to crawl to it through Snooks's bed room into the ketchen. Snooks have *one* of just what he need: one fork, one spoon, one plate...the phone agin and I pulled myselfs up to the dish counter and take the receiver from the hook. I couldnt hold it with my one hand so I needed to cup it with both of my hands and lean it on my shoulder and push it near next of my head: 'Who this? Huh? ' The voice on the other end says: 'This is Lester...' The last name cause a trembling in me, humbleness's that I aint should owed to nobody but God. And I aint floundering near next of the gate of apologys cause I aint met *The Lord,* yet, so I caint know the humbleness of that day, but I can says that the feeling come'd over me, forced me to hug that phone and lean to the counter: 'O, Yeah Mr. —' He stopped my words: 'Is John Wright (that's Coolie) there? ' 'O, no sir, ' — my talk come'd from nowheres — 'he aint. But if you would to leave a thought I'd surely pass it to him when he come'd in.' My talk seemed angelic. Mr. Lester: 'Well, my drummer has not shown up for our engagement and I need a drummer for tonight. If John comes home soon, I will be at the "Z" club for a while. He can reach me there. Thank you...' He might done says good bye or something but I be emotional at his *Thank you* coming at me and I just hung up the phone and slow'd myselfs to the floor with that music in my ear. I crawled to long sides but this time I aint got the strength to climb onto it so I just lays there.

Help me somebody
Help me...
somebody

'Goddamn! Nobody stopped, Uncle Nough. Nobody stopped. Shake your head in: Nobody's.' That's my Los Angeles.

Everything I wants to do I gots to prove myselfs first. I been so busy trying to prove so much to everybody that when the Lord comes I wont have anything to show I'll says when He ask bout me: 'Ask them.'

Part III

Scribblings of Love

To them damn gull-birds, I promise something if they taken no notice.

1. Nivea

They aint even not have to tell me cause I knowd it. Un huh. I known cause of the day we be in the wood's-grass and you aint let me to rub play on your stomach. Well-water-concern rise up on my fore face deep down tween my eyes concern: put my mind to imaginings — a week long or more, it were — and give my heart reason fer the haunt-hurts.

O I spent them week days in a posession *power*, being round me and I were let to move only as that *power* wished. I spent days in the all emotion state, trying not to let on to anyone. There were moments with my head spent and tween my legs; *hot,* come to the bottom of my feet and I wants to scream out loud but to do that, I gots to fight with myselfs fer the privilage. I studied hard on what to do; what we'd do ...

And the sun in me were you everything were you, in it. I took the thought that you praise be! were with mine's insides of yourselfs. And you were not gonna tell me but I knowd it were coming

sure as dead decaying leaves helps the trees to give!

I knowd it were coming my eyes aint knowd it. I watched you close all them days your walk; to see if you comed bow-legged, to make room fer it to drop. Your front (to side) to see if it had begun to pull your hind along yet. But all my imaginings be too early. I imagines lots — couldnt help — and everytime my eyes be getting into something, I'd blink way even the image of evidence thought itselfs!

NIVEA

Do your look
make mens melt
pour me all on ice

cause you a
cold cold cold cold
cold cold pretty looking
wo-man

In the woods I'd dance round, drunk of no rhythm and read from my palms, pushed together as a book of poem words or even the bible, all the letters of preciousness I would've to write you since I aint be in the way of saying: 'I loves you, darling.' I recite it loud as sure on account of the world dont minds when your weakness be written within your heart and when your words am so sweet that the bee is try to git at your lips rather than land bout the flower.

O let me tell you
what it's like to BE,
when you silly with honeyness!

Lord! the animals, rather than is scattered by fear, be come'd out to see *curious me!* and consider on man, surrendered to sweet ONENESS...

...makes you pull your arms close in on yourselfs 'YEAR! ', your bodyselfs shake in giggles spread them arms out to fly but you does movement akin to the place *where you from, ages ago* — I means way back afore your memories history; and the whole woods come'd a cone of sound   Lordinization! ! !

I ask the trees to 'be silent' of this day
not to let the wind pry it from them.
To them damn gull-birds, I promise something
if they taken no notice.

Here I be talking and letting my heart run-flow to yours and like the preacher putting it over the pulpit, I done my selfs like-wise. I be thinking that you were getting it and it be coming back to me cause your head be bobben and nodding thus and so   your eyes close to add dimention and I'm moved to press on into the freedom of your *under-standing* as you ask: 'What time is it? ' HELL!   there aint no time. I took the thought that we'd reached it!   That some kind of some place   I closed my eyes and soared   only to come back to your blank and drained face. O, you stole it from me. Outdoor women aint got no shame.

she: 'It aint your baby so you aint got a damn thing to worry bout Strutter.'

Strutter (as if not hearing her): 'Honey, I been taken the bad wall paper offen the walls, burning the old paint off the wood and just making ready the old place just for...'

she: 'Listen, man, I dont know. What would people say. What I got to give you in return!   What you want me for anyway.'

Strutter: 'Well, now, shit. It aint like we done happen up on each other like the first moment of anything fool all, but tighten much to me in this: we found each self in each! damn it. We filled the space tween us and your fingers dug many a thought deep in the ground out back in the woods it be *my* name that uprooted the grass even not if it were your own grip that tore it from the ground! AARON! O Aaron, you screemed to whimpers and flung the grass-dirt and shit on my bareness...'

she: 'I ask Aaron Brown if he knowd you and he say, yeah.'

But Strutter aint never knowd Aaron Brown but thought: She wanted me so bad she got her a man with my name and done confused my child with him.

she: 'and besides, how you gonna play music out here? Aint nobody want to hear your mess. I aint sure I wants to have a baby. I'm got lots of funning to do. Me and babies aint no future for me if I has it...'

Strutter'd find himselfs frowning at the taste of salt on tears licked from the corner of his lips: 'We got our hands on the door knob but you wouldnt talk to me cause: *"of the expression on your bottom lip,"* shit. *Someday,* is happiness and my whole face gonna be my mouth smiling SWEAR TO GOD! You is my quiet, I be your: *"mine! "'* He remember'd Nivea went way from his face. She aint want to see his words come'd.

aint nothing washed way
with the drops slip dripping
from my chin

they's a conductor
to what I tries to
forgits

— Nivea's face come'd to the center of his mind — 'O Lord, I forgits, easily, why I come'd to my knees. Lord, please stop the pictures I wants to talk with You sure! ' Strutter folded his arms tight stiffened himself/Released! and he tries to rock like other arms be bout him, a sway from within someone else's bosom. Choir singing sister's, mighty big on religion shouting would give a fine sight-thought on the mood in which Strutter be posed. His head shake shudder in the way of the quivers: 'I means to tell You that I needed a friend and at the last of the darkness I forgot that *day brought news;* I forgot to talk with You; I didnt cry out or ask Your permission but I declared alone to come calling. I heard the sisters and deacons of the shroud, speak clearly talk bout appointed conclusions and such like, but I aint pay no mind.

'I went to moaning the tune my mama went to You with...

I will see the Great King
in all his Glory...

'I aint so right bout the tune but I knowd to remember the words. I be moved to depths. The *swells's up* in me, be a test and trouble to my mind. Now Lord, I thought-planned to sleep on over to You. So I took many as all these quieten pills to aspire on. I took the plastic kind of bag, done placed it over my head, tied it round my neck and lay out to do travel. BUT AINT I MADE THE SHAME AWFULLNESS MIS-CARE! I aint made enough sinse of my plan to blow my breath in that bag, puts that bag in the water afore and press fer to see holes and 'scapage. So there me and the bag be breathing together...from prune head to balloon thing.

O I cuss mumbles lots

'I aint want to say much in that way cause I knowd I were coming to You, Lord.

'Then I tried to hold-pinch my nose inside the bag but that aint no good to allow me to *sleep* over to You and I gots damn mad – ah, excuse me, as ever – and I started to cuss, Bad! roll and suck the bag some, in and out of my mouth. I fought with my head. THIS AINT WHAT I PLANNED – NO NOT TO ARRIVE IN NO DISTURBANCE! Bout that time them pills come'd to working and I passed out. My dead-done-been-gone mama with other presences, stay stood bout and watched motioned to me "wait awhile dont cross over just yet."

'When I come'd woke, I'd forgot what I'd done done and so I be plenty scared with this thing all bout my face. I pulled at it and tried to scream but sucked up the bag in my mouth. I done tear it off along with some hair in a minute and rolled out of my bed on the floor. My whole head were wet with sweat and my hair be in a itch-scratch.

I might've been a smarter like old Miss Prims is done to die, and just called all the house for rent ads in the town folk's newspaper, asking if the house come'd with a gas stove; till she found one.

'O, Lord, is I forgived? '

Nivea went sick when she come'd from the hospital. She were thin from the start of her days and though thin things come'd in style in these days, *thin* had marked days in her time. So as to be aspected, she taken with what doctoring caint work on and come'd the distance in the middle of a coughin spell. Moanin be sparse cause she aint been knownced fer her *good* ways but those that didnt or werent use of carrying gossip did attend her wake so she be laid way in courtesy.

'Well,' Strutter pulled a kleenex from the box by his cot and cried into some snot on to it: 'I been thinking on justice and how there aint much in this world.' He wiped his mouth cause a fly flown close. 'You know...(to nobody)...I got arrested *the other day* fer driving a car *I brought over in town once.* The police says, I gots no business coming with this car across the lines with no licenses plate, But I says I just got it at the man's shop and I be just taken it home. Aint that far I need a license plate fer? Cept, that dont make no difference and I got the ticket fer proof. Now at the time I works fer the post folks and you aint suppose to git no police nothing on you or it's out of the job. Here? So I shoots pool with Judge Jones, the *first* we sent to the bench out our way; and I told him over the table what come'd to me and how worried I be bout my job. I says: Man, what I gots to do? If I goes to jail, my job is had it. The Judge Jones, leaned over the table and hit the side pocket and set himselfs up fer a easy run of it: "Aaron, (smiling cause he made the run) You aint got to worry bout nothing, boy; NOTHING! I aint suppose to tell you a thing but I'm winning (ha! ha!) and you aint even not (the judge spoke home-like at *home)* got no lawyer, so beins as I can help, I will. But you dont tell-a-whisper to nobody. Here? Now, you did break the law. Dont strange-up on me bout that: you done . But it aint no big thing and you didnt mean to do it. I know that. So you go to court and tell your story and I mean tell the truth. The presiding judge will see you is honest and he'll have to fine you but it wont be that much and you wont go to no jail." Then he held my shoulder, reached right and touched me, grab'd my shoulder like the preacher do and bow'd his head. Man, I payed him fer winning the game and some extra fer the releaving sighs I carried all the way to the court house the next tuesday. I asked the judge what the fine would cost and he says: *thirty-five dollars;* and thats all I brung with me. I come'd near nervous when I entered the court house but, *Lord, save us, do do protec and comfort* fer on the bench were *my buddy,* the JUDGE!

'I know'd I be all right now. I made promises and thanked the Lord, even fer the things to come. The first case were called by the bailiff: "The court calls Madam Lil Turn, to the bench." There were movement in the room when this woman with hair uncombed come'd up the way and through the gate. She wore a pink-faded dress and house slippers with no straps scraping up the sound of her approach and sleep were all over her as like she done been pulled from bed to come to the court. There be wonderment and laughins and the judge hit the gavel on the bench and come'd out of his robe: 'Who is the arresting officer in this case? "

'Madam Lil Turn, were the fine-ness pros. on the street and the good judge know'd it but the woman *before* him could not only be THE MADAM LIL TURN but no self respecting officer could ever MISTAKE *this* woman fer a *prostitute* and he asked the grey suited man beside her: "How in the world did you come to approach *this* woman ..." There be some question as to the officer's condition and were he drinking afore and the judge thanked the woman who aint says a word yet (fer coming at this inconvenience) and dismissed the case.

'I know'd I were *in!* O Baby! I were damn happy into fraid when the bailiff shout: "The court calls Aaron Strutter... (he read my case as I come'd farward, my 'Hello' in my jaws)...How do you plead? " "GUILTY. YOUR WORSHIP." I shout-hollered fer the whole court room to know'd I were honest.

' "Fifty dollars." and a flat on flat blam of the gavel be the period of it. "Next case." He says all that and never raised his god-damn head to see who I be. I were stun'd. The thirty-five dollars went limp in my hand and I went into the droops like the grass in my sink do when they cuts off the water. This screaming went on inside me: look up judge, buddy, it's me. And the breaking of the ball on the pool table up like he'd heard it from the WHERES: 'Well, pay the bailiff. Pay the bailiff! " I says: "I aint gots but thirty-five dollars...SIR." He aint even look at me just at the bailiff and point: "Take this man to jail."

'Good thing the turn-key be a friend of a taxi driving friend of mine. He called our friend and he come'd pay the fine. So I knows there's a *Understanding,* when I went right on over to that house and took mine and Nivea's baby and brung it home where I made a place fer it. Cause aint no justice in this world   you gots to do what you knows. At 46, I know'd that fer sure.'

Billy:
Hey man, you hear that the Strutter done stole Nivea's baby?

Clyde:
Yeah. What gonna be done? Everybody too shocked to think.

'Gone, gone. The welfare picked him from me! ' Fer the next twenty years, Strutter'd had his hands on his head everytime he thought on the boy but he werent not to see him again: 'One thing, he aint been here long enough to git no use of his name; I just called him Son, most. Gone.'

Gull-birds say:

Strutter tween
wishin, backed up in him:
come'd believing and
son, lingered

I *sort of felt it.* I didnt knowd it a first but I just sought and felt it.

And I started just screaming. Just anywheres; just screaming; cause I felt he be dead   and sho nough I come'd home   and he were.

I caint put myselfs in mind of the scene no more. But I wanted to do somethin nice. So I had to send him to Brunswick; I had to send my baby's body to Brunswick and have him cremated.

In a few days they tol me to come and git him   and I took what money I had and I went and sat in the train station   and as I had sometime to wait, I guess I doze'd   anyway, somebody stole my money; a hundred and twenty five dollars on the day I were gonna collect my baby's ashes, somebody stole my money from me. So I made the trip with that on my mind and I thought I shouldnt of come'd today. But worst of all, when I got to the place they gave me my baby's body in one of them   them kraft jars   the big kind   that have salad dressing in it. It be just, my baby's ashes just in a jar and it in a old bare wood box that somebody have carried somethin in. They just handed it at me. Well, what they did is when I tol them I aint had no money, they says: 'Just a minute.' They says: 'Well, have to take it *out* of the urn.'   And that's how he come'd to be in the kraft jar.

And I brought my baby's body back here and I took him home and I went down by the creek, the stream that run on our property   and I poured the ashes on the stream and some went away but others sunk to the bottom cause it were all at once I did it.

And I says a prayer;
but I aint want to pray much so I tried to make up a poem.
And I could see the reflection of my baby's ashes on the bottom at the creek and some would float-trail away ev'ry now and then. A STIRRINS. My baby's bones were at the bottom of the creek. I COULD SEE THEM THERE; and I says another poem.

My prayers ascend to arch   never complete.

It's the damn inner voices that gots they way. They interrupt, suggest and flash pictures over my prayers so that I must sometimes – when I catches this – pray with my eyes open to be more truthful;   yet they do most times win and *I am embarrassed* when speaking to the Lord be overshadowed and like a broken disc   I am caught on the gaze of rememberings and thoughts that stumble me, still me from my purpose.

2. Son

A mad wind, a kind that's been named after womens, forced a horn sound-thought through a hole'd out dead arm branch of the old oak tree on the top hill bove Strutter's place. Echo hollow be its sound moaning high bove the sustained drone of a swarm of honey bees. In his front yard were winter and a no-milk-boney-hipped cow which lapped salt in *'the puble of Aunt Sarah's eye.'*

Strutter see'd all this from hind his front door. The great door, its windows to put someone in mind of a upright ice cube tray, stood tween Strutter and the world. There's inside, a sunken place round that fine door. It be the place where he most stood and done his thinking. It also be where Strutter's son waited on him coming in from work. There aint no account of the years ago but the Strutter's son be six of age and some afore the child were gone. Strutter been tied in that spot ever since. The varnish finish done peeled way and the floor dips-sink from the man's weight pressing to the years of crying on to the bare board wood; him standing as ever in the same thinking spot: looking through one of them glass square panes and trying to put his child's image outside mongst dressed in some blue dark blue overthings thus a image – the child's – standing, with his little hands covering his eyes, like shutter things, in peakin fashion; knee up in old rust leaves and frost wet.

Now the child were want to 'pee' so he danced, pigeon-toe'd – knees near knocking each other and look,

the gull-birds
swear

...with all the life of a little train puffing out its breath-steam waiting to move, but glued even in motion to that spot. Strutter, to speak humbly talking out loud: 'Go git on in here and pee, boy! ' to which the gull-birds did no comment nor contradict just listen.

Strutter: 'Lord, Will it! ' to understand the boy might obey...'O he be with me' but the man squint-look and the image were gone.

Well, who can bring
a same echo back?

O Lord, let, to
tell this truth

Strutter, shaken put himselfs a dream thought. In this vision he imagized the hind of himselfs in a great over-rap and cap with heavy boots – that's right – he'd stand that man, who's back be to him himselfs own back! out in that frost-wet-same-spot-vision where of the boy's image been afore like to cover over. He caint see the boy cause *his* image protec the boy even from himselfs: 'High darn it! why not to be closer! ' He look way to pride in his doings STRUTTER'S LAUGHINS BE THE DANCE – sweat drippings to in that sunken place where he, head shaking 'shucks 'n sure nough' stand bobbing til he need remind himself, from hind the door. He beam out the glass pane agin – Lord! still there – bow'd his head thought on they walks took from winter through spring to winter ... he spoke to these thoughts:

'I went tired on the River Folk's place property. My heart were a sure noise   it beat too heavy loud   and I tried to cover over it like we does when we takes show of the allegence. Felt like I come'd the distance   cept my mind be on you, son. I took to resting   sit myselfs quite   next of a tree to push some snow round and think on.

'There's cracked glass in the fine door – your mama liked – where when I enters, old dust rise; be put to framing your nose and lip prints   stopped on the cold glass pane the day you were shut in with the flu and tried to lick kiss the window sweat way. I can see it plain even the outsides, them days when you be knee up in old leaves winter wishes; sniffling.'

O, He werent to
feeling it though

Strutter knowd not to curse cause his boy might hear him   so cried aloud; the scream going into the cracks of everywhere.

O moan a prayer!

Should it ever come'd to be discribed, says: 'He melted to his knees, his hand's fingers reached to individual window seals in the door but not grabbing, just as a jester!'

Let it be knownced that way

His head bow'd as tears moved on his cheeks to a place and runs backwards a ways to make drops...and drops...so be the running from his nose. He press a finger to its right side and the first sense of profanity burst from the other side. What didnt hit the floor, he wiped away with his hand and dry on his overhauls, in back, near the bed in his knee; then put the heel of his right thumb to wiping his eyes of tears and sweat.

Strutter, on his knees and pull-crawl to the small window pane at the bottom right of the door In *need* he reach to kiss the old lip and tongue print smear of his son's but as he come'd upon the pane his breath be made solid and seen to cloud-obscure the image on the pane. Strutter moves *to wipe away his breath:* 'O Shit! ' ... but suddenly jerks way his hand fer fear of wiping way – even the memory – his son's evidence lefted.

He set back, fiddles with the floor cracks and begins to mumble. He hums some old hymnal, reminder of shackles chains and be to a trance of himselfs his eyes glazed of tears: 'O Lord...' his words ascend but to curb a imaginary arch best realized in the spirit of an old tree breached bent and refused the upward Strutter's prayer is lost in thoughts and out loud talk to his son:

'I walk at night and pretend you be walking next of me so I talks to you. My lips takes on the shape of your lips and the words I says be yours (the ones I members) with the sound of your voice in my silence. I'd git so caught up once'd I spoken out and stopped short; it shook me really did and I looked round to see if somebody done heard it and continued in quiet, amongst myselfs. There come'd a night I be walking in deep snow I retraced my path and made new steps aside mine, gone afore, in the same direction ceptin this time I played the artist; designed trot-happy moves and let my shadow, throw'd from

a oil lamp light cast itselfs over them first foot marks; I ... up'd went
you   swung'd you round   out in air   like to loose you, *go!*   and
listen for your giggle – uh huh – til my hands come'd cold and I
watched them into my pockets   watched my shadow bend'd over
as the crow do   a slow steppin in hard times.

'O well, I werent not having a love affair with myselfs...but I is been left
to my imagination.'

...and if Strutter be seen from top of the stairs in that old house, he
looked to be in a deep well.

His hands cupped: 'Linger with me, son.'

'Tears map your features, fer
my fingers to follow, from
my brow   down
to where the crying
flows at my chin

and I be reduced;
touching myselfs,
to see your
image

tears
have taught me
your face

I be sometimes crying
in my fist'

and fer moments he gaze – hoarse hums:

'Your cheeks and chin cupped
in my hands my thumbs moved
to press tears from your
eyelashes sensitive
all the time to your eye's movement
from hind my touch

but hind my touch be me
and it's my hands that knowd
your face

whilst holding my own,
buried and tear-stained.

I members taking a tear
from your cheek
and rubbing it dry tween my thumb
and my finger

then snapping them together
to a "aint nothing to it, little man" smile

but hind my touch be me
and it's my hands that knowd

your face
whilst holding my own.'

Lord! Strutter spit
at his shadow

and watch a spider to quiet:

'I members us
going to the creek
one day

I knowd you
to be fraid of snakes so,
I took a stick along

seems it were
down the stretch
close to Juka's cave

at a moment so sudden
my whole body were flush
and warm
and numb
with

my anticipizion
I shouted:
"Hold it! "

and rushed
into
beating   a dead tree limb.

Guess I didnt even
look up

just stuck my hand out and
motioned:
"Come on, boy." '

His fingers slow-pull
tears from his cheek
as he quick jerk a breath

'You aught to
write me
something, son.

O dont worry
about it being
too short

it didnt take
long to kill
the Lord;

but, see
we never
forgot it.'

This bitter damn burden   bitter damn burden   to exist here and be totally unthought of   and to have your every thought to be against all you fear and believe to be true. 'Bitter damn burden.' Exiled in my mind fer years   'BITTER DAMN BURDEN! '

Strutter were fully dressed   just come in from the outsides and slowly move, like a crying man,   across   to the corner of his cot-bed, and removing his butterfly panama hat – flips it – lifts his body down on one knee, the hat flopping to the center of the cot   his arm, wedge like, rest and support himselfs from the end of the bed. 'Bitter Damn Burden! ' as if he'd begun to like saying it and in this feeling he went right way to mumbling a prayer: 'O Lord...good Friend of mines... Destiny, O no!   SCARES   O the scares what am. What be I spose to ask fer? '

His mind flash pictures of memories   fast to him   his mumbling stops as he shakes his head   tries to shake his mind off '...Forgit the prayer...' He grabs his forehead   pauses   then begins to massage his temples. Flashes.

In a kitchen near a ice box frig: Strutter's arms wrapped round this woman's body, bare from the waist up   and she be warm. His hands were at first, a part of her. Pressing. Squeezing. Searching and counting back bones. He could ask fer her thoughts and trust she be not so mad cause in his asking, she'd know they werent his.

But he thought better on it and watched-followed   a crack that had climbed the wall into the ceiling and began   were pulled into rhythm sounds coming from a phonograph in another room. His hands played un-known tunes; pat out a counter rhythm up and down the bone column of her bare back like the saxophone player do, but she dont take a notice. The two of them, answering each's moans, moved in circles bringing wonderings to his mind '...and how long this this time...' and his eyes lite on the kitchen sink...so much mud dirt that grass be growing in there! He'd think: 'This woman's hands aint fer cleaning' hugged her closer more like to protect her from that sink and stopped the circling so she might not be let to see it...

...his tongue caught the
taste of salt at the edge corner of his lips...

Strutter's room open'd up on him.
He began a prayer again:
'O Lord,
Destiny, O no.'

3. Pemba Jade

And when that part of him that makes fer his genteelness done gone, he turned bitter cursted 'ON HIGH'... Say, he been *robbed* and *took from!* He done this bitterness and sayings til he went courting agin. This time she be a woman from the East Hill area and of the River Folks, out back. He'd say: 'Liquorice and pigtails done always be a test fer me. The River Folks' women be of both thoughts and be in the image of doe-selfs Dears! ...that makes the heart to...LORD! She say:

Sweep-by-up
me heart
O be Jesus!
I loves you boy

Old Aaron say: 'Pemba Jade, were the essence of the doe-deer in spring planting time.' and that it were this Miss Pemba Jade, slim line black River Folks woman that made him – fer folks know'd him in a different way – to hide out in his bar; leap and giggle blushness up in himselfs among the hay.

O be Jesus!
I loves you boy

Old Aaron'd sing late at night, come'd home from courting:

Pemba jade be her name
an opalescence
she wore it all over
and she looked just the same

year (yell it out!)
after year!

AND in my memory she tol me lies like
proof on her cheeks from
the wet in her eyes
to-make-me-pull-my-toes
together in curls
and pat out the boogie in my heart
for the girl

Opalescence
Pemba Jade WHO! (shout it)
Lord! Cant close her door
before she give me some
lovin

(laughins)

and roll back in the hay his hands would fall on his face and hold that big apple smile of the trash mans' when he git paid, 'Wine Face!

He often heard to says:

'I knows I be a sinner. My biggest *sin* is my wife. She looks some owly at me and natters a bit to apologize but I says to her: You knows, when the sun shines the rock gots to get hot! And she'd smile a sun...come'd right off'n Pemba Jade's jaws and cheeks.'

'O Lord! '

Then grabbed it! to her palm and let loose a: 'Yelp-yip-muh! ' That's when she goes into her circlings. Just starts at her right elbo and moves herselfs in that right direction til she come-meet the place she come'd from.

Strutter'd hear Pemba Jade's voice-tellings:

'I come'd early on saturdays. Come'd in the fore light and wait in the just-afore-the-night-ends noises. O no, I werent not afraid, I knowd Strutter'd be round soon. I'd feel the presence of his approachins and I knowd too, he *had* to go to where he be coming: right cross the pond there and ground his fishing pole to rest all day. There were a difference: in turn, I be gone to sleep whilst waiting fer him. And *DONE,* sometimes that a gull-bird fly near a crying it be just like the "WHERES" asking me to pay a notice. I'd jerk: "ugh" aware quite some frowny, raising my brow my gaze-up picked-cross to his image in the pond; then THERE in the morning blue of hazes's just made, be Aaron, sipping-slups of hummings on his own thoughts bout how good the firmament be.

'Shortness of breath? *Oooo, dont waste your money!* fer sure it come'd; everywhilst when I see'd him. I palm-pats-hold: *"O my! "* my cheeks; holds in that: something th'scoming from...fer even not the "WHERES" aint fer to see my shy shame bloom. He knowd I so touched caint look him straight! With my head bowed, my eye hair makes fer blurry come'd like I be peering out from under myselfs into that there pond where his image be til he chunk a rock in it and FORCE, come'd my cheek to rub close my shoulder: slide-slowing up to meet his eyes. *Oooo, dont waste your money, honey!* *Be Jesus,* it fer sure. Shortness of breath?' (laughins)

...and Strutter laughins into begins telling this story to himselfs in his play-Pemba Jade voice, out loud:

O she told it
more better

'Now, Aaron love to fish. Most to truth, Aaron, true loved beer and fishing come'd a way of doing it *DRINKING!* Yeah. Hah? But he took to fishing cause aint no work in it the way he done it. Just put the line of bate in the water ...not throwing it, he hang it light like; then forced the pole to at a angle in the soft wetnesses of ground off the side where the weeds grows to curl-curves like girly bangs and leaves off in not quite mud-dirt scooping into the pond. Oooo and he'd find "that spot" to stretch himselfs out near next of a tree and open; open up on "home-firmament-tastens" all day til the man be with blur'd sunset in his eyes and the snake'd cross through on the water to the west.

' "Jollyin", it be when he spoke on it, tho, it werent not no fasination bout it cause he usely dont catch a thing. Ceptin, one day the line come'd pulled and begun to swim bout in circles with 'plup' sounds now and then. Aaron, up'd and spilt: "Damn" his tastens, pulling the line-thing in. He just jerk up of the water and quick come'd a fish still in the struggle. The thing come'd swinging cross straight at Aaron and he, *glazed!* grab-stagger at it to *miss* and on the swing

back — I swear boy — the fish slap'd Aaron! SWEAR IT! The fish's tail come'd flapping with a meant aim: hauled off and slap'd a mess of scales right up side the man's face. A horse were there you should of seen it scared. Aaron, mad'd up fast, slammed the damn fish on the ground and come'd to stomping on it afore you could tell what the family of the fish be. SWEAR IT!

'See, Aaron, go bare foot near all the time; so you can visualize the meaning of it, if you take my point. Hah? Aaron...a scale be in his eye and up to then he kept his lips doubled inside his mouth and mute: "muh's" companied the stomp. *COME'D!* Aaron, stomp'd: he stomp'd the spine bone of the fish right up in his foot. Lord! it swole'd. The man hollored — alerted all the wildlife in the vicinity and the snake crossed *back!* To see. O Aaron, walk'd bout. He be so mad he, tippy-skipping, crippled on down the road to town to the fish market — hit the owner man over the head and went in to tearing the place *up.* The police come'd and caught him, cussing and stomping a frozen perch and this be how Aaron, come'd to be in jail a time.'

Strutter'd look way with 'Damn' on his lips...

on sundays, mongst
the grass — I done
scribblings in his
blue suede shoes

P.J.

Is you ever have dreamed in a dream bout someone you know'd and in that dream the person done made you mad? Pemba, done. Of Aaron. She had one of them nightmares woke up mad at him and moved way while he be at work. He never know'd a thing no why's no nothing.

Old Aaron'd talk to himselfs: 'There's got to be some truth to this woman I call by the name I do. Sh'so soft-goin and saving of her words, to put the thought: *Precious!* on my mind when I pray-mention her to the Lord. She say: 'Yeah,' by taken in the breath which cause the ear to lift concern'd as to her well being and bringing bout my *all* to her attention: 'Is you touched unwell, Honey Miss? ' and I seen puzzlement as her ears moves towards her brow bout the concern she see'd in my eyes and a frown come'd instead of the words she almost spoken cept fer I so quick to loosen my thought: 'Naw. You all right, aint yah? ' ...to which she sucked in a 'Yeah.'

It be near next of the custom I be used in hearing but in her voice it become'd the feeling of lace curtains when wind-blown'd-swing-up into mama's parlor room to fall back round my shoulder and brush drag at my cheek, a bit tickley-warm; make things rise in yah! I'd play like it were somebody come'd to put they arms bout me in days when nobody called me, *mine.*

'Yeah.' – with the breath sucked in.

I been partialized to the sound ever since.

Part IV

Old Aaron

Death done put me in mind of where I done come'd.

1. Strutter

His choices in life had shaped him in the curve of the grass cycle, worn him dull and left him inverted, accused — he believed the gull-birds spoke of him often in gossipy tones — and he looked marked of rust ash at the eyelashes his crying ...they say: larve could live in the junk of his tears. And the man sweat *so much!* no matter what time of the year. Everything he wore were of the same scent. The children say he aught to bottle that scent call it, 'Strutter Musk,' and sell it to the slum lords to spread-round the row houses and ethnic areas during the tourist season. For *authenti-something* they called it.

Yet, he still managed a poverty molded proudness when he felt anyone be making a notice of him. Got right dignified ... or is it *some dignified?*

Strutter say he from way back; 1800 and something and lived this long on his mind methods and attractive bald head. He say: 'As a boy I done this I got my baldness one day whilst playing in a short weed area with one tree known as THE JUNGLE. It were down the water-road from my home, facing the sea. We round there use to play with every-anything; and one day we found a half empty oil can down by the sea shore and brung it to our jungle. For days we be setting fires and dancing round them until we'd used up what's left in the can. Well, we just dropped it in the jungle and went off in the somewheres. And I forgits, but some later, me and Boo Boy — that's Mr. Timothy Snooks, a white gentleman, dead, twenty years 'go, and be with the gull-birds, undoughtedly — Anyway, we found the can and I were some interested to know if there be any oil left cornering that can. Boo Boy stood right over me as I knee'd myself and helt one eye at the hole of the can but darkness aint help me see a thing so I lite a match, throw'd it in there and looked in...'

'They say the can blow'd up...'

the gull-birds know
for sure fer to talk
of it

Strutter, EXpanded off his knees up, shouting; even seemed like he come'd out of the can! Eyebrows and hair were gone! looked just like the jinni and run'd LORD! STOPPED THE WIND! his right arm lapped over his whole head the hand digging, dogging into his jaw whilst his other hand be holding from his chin and half covering, like finger flesh bars, a mess of tears and what seemed of a holy sanctified endless cry.
only gull-birds lost
out to sea in great storms
come'd to sound
the same

He'd loss all sense of his where or *how be it was* and the usual tenseness that identify him by his walk weren't present. O, he still favored his right leg but he seemed pulled along, some magical! He were carrying a yellow white, sweat crued on it stained, old panama straw hat in his left hand perch resting, butterfly like on his hipside; a cane supporting from the other hand as he bent over most spiral in the way of the fiddle head's growth following some ants. The image of the old man were in all his possessions. Cept, that cane. Well, it shake as the old man but seemed it had a will of its own – like the 'well finder's stick' do when it point out water neath us – it sometimes digging in the grown-dirt, next of them ants, LINES, what scares and confuses them and put the old man to apologizing for it: 'Ah, s'cuse Shhhhhhhhhhhh. I aint mean fer to bring fuss to your workins.'

His face were clean shaven (as possible) and very dark, cept'n for a shiny scar (razor no doubt) that come'd from his throat up by his left ear and into his lighter skinned bald head the top of his head catching the sun's rays and giving the appearance of as he be wearing a priest's cap. He be covered in a camel's hair cassimere coat of some age a size too big but his from the beginning; he'd only lost weight. The coat hid all but the ballon'd shape of his overhaul cuffs stuffed into winter wool socks and ageless brogan 'stompers' construction boots.

Didnt even take notice of the six foot high furrowed tin sheets that made walls, fence and doors into the city dump just follow them ants' work line — head down — right in thru up to and scatters (as in fright): 'Filthy Damn flies! ' ...waving his cane mongst them and discovering they business and the destination of the ants to what's left of a dog chewed rat, ceased making it.

'Mercy blossom! what you gonna steal from the junk mens? '

In thot motions slow as yesterday's bowel movement to come, something dawn on him — due maybe to one of them flies slamming up side his forehead and in a wound down voice: 'How I in this place? ' ...him stretching his eyes upwards under closed lids transparent all color spots put him more to an illusion til some loud laughins make real the shock of 'comin back! '

Strutter, jerk up!   and near flip over backwards: 'Obie? ! ' He shaded his brow and look a long question   the illusion giving way to recognition   then humiliation; but covered: 'Obie? Well, ah, I guess I acts like I be with a contusion   mindless...' All smiles, he relaxes, put his straw panama a top his head   then faking it, stiffens up and struts over in Obie's direction   his construction boots reaching for secure ground – the tensness being back with each step: 'Them ants done lead me in here and right up to where they's after' ...he points the cane back of him – in no direction – to show somewhere...'them flies and the sight of Death puts me in mind of where I done come'd; your junk yard!   huh! ' He reached to Obie and look him straight on in the face.

'Strutter? Old man, you still trailing bugs? ! '

Obie's concern bein more of a put-on-down-cism; his eyes telling the truth of it.

Gull birds been disturbed off some garbage cause of Obie's laughin racket   they puts periods to all sound and takes attention with they shout cries. Strutter, sat down where the dog named 'Trouble,' went his wants earlier. The old man thot of the rain the day afore.

little bubbles
burst-popping
in gum squeaks

He were old bone   lived off eating the air   reached the age when he'd step on all the cracks in the sidewalk. And when asked, he'd kindly reply: 'I'm a old time, yeah sir.'

At a bugle call he'd *stiffen up* and prance-hide his years. The past'd urge up in his blood what young womens'd wonder about were left'd in him to do. Before a crowd he'd magic'd up a selfs that presented us with a *sho* more liquid in its flow and grace than the peacocks' tracks and tell all about on how he got his way in life.

He'd say-sing: 'Here's how I payed my rent.' Laughins and a opening dance sway; he'd draw you in...

Tell the man nicely
in the image
so the tale might
lead him come

Toe dance and step-jerk
a little back away
showing the palms of your
hands

'Now, now.'

that's it –
VIVID!

leave him
uphilled in his faith
rare, like

WHITE CROWS

O how we delights to go from his thoughts on this subject to our quiet place and thinks on the imaginations come up from the feelings we be left'd with.

Lord, bless my right pocket cause that's all I can give you today.

2. Honor Believe

Strutter, like a rat, done made a hole, eye high, next of a corner in his room. Ever since he heard life come from hind the other side he'd scratched (to his fantasies) a little mortar way when he thought the sound wouldnt be of notice. Afore the hole were done, he visioned and danced and made promises to himselfs bout the woman – he knowd fer sure – who snored at night: 'My to God! I have heard through the walls old hum'd up melodies, coming with shortness of breath-broken rhythms, slow shush-put-pull walkings across your room: stockings dragging on the board, eh? and always I be let to filling the space of my thoughts: such music to linger with and put me to sways. The wish in my heart makes fer a turn in me and I reach to touch the sympathy of the past. This *Sympathy*, I hiss and Plead to "SEE TO IT I just go and be with the friends." My pulse be of a rush much like I done taken of a beer.

'I'm swelled. Your foot steps speak on the bare board: your mood; your decision. I done heard you stomp fer more heat huh! even not stomp fer quiet and the pipes would at times answer: Clank, Clank; a anger and a *up yours.* Then you'd pause... E-ve-ry-night, the pause and I'd open my arms and vision you come'd by me fer comfort: scoot over squeeks to clasp my cheeks, smear-kiss my nose away. O, I done made much of the pause. My imaginings see you mouthing what you wont says and your fingers shake searching fer to make the fist; interrupted as you'd scoot over creaks to springs that give-tense and says you wish to sleep. TO SWEET HEAVEN! I *cuss* the loneliness you'd leave me in when you'd sleep. And I couldnt.

'In my bed I'd bounce – as I could, eh? – a thought to wake you and give you to thinks: "That fellow be having one good time over there! " But that's not so good a thing to do cause my bed is old. "My Dear? Have you ever heard the noise? "'

Strutter's thoughts mingled and confused and he closed his eyes in 'No's...' Tears'd cleanz his soul he believed that and gathered in on himselfs fer to explode: he might come'd to cry out hard but no sound. It were like standing afore a cave and trying to suck all the air from it in one massive-slur'd hiccup. Tho, some slobbers run'd round his chin in his hands and he cupped them to his face, rubbing them in cause no real tears done shone... and he laugh'd: 'I remembers touching your shyness whilst you fumbled round and protests: the air is just *out there* helping everybody. It dont make no *friend!* Well, we is of but we aint like the air, baby. I be born with the ambition to be clean all my lifes. But now I have to die dirty cause of my job. You know? A little touch here, a rub there and always I be having to wipe my hands on no place. See? – with disgust – On my chest. If I be standing, the sides of my pants wherever! And it collects. The air dont make no friends but I'm here I collects. You see, I needs.'

Strutter shook his head from a shudder of ...a tear did come'd. He talked out to the *'Wheres':* 'Come take me fer a walk. Pat my hands guide me by my shoulder, help my step and bend me so I mights sit down. I leaves my house open, dont worry bout the door. I put my keys way long ago less I "come'd the distance" and some person be of need to git in my house. That's smart – even now: so come on.'

'And when times come'd bad, our love stayed on the road, crowded round us whilst others backed odd and off. Sometimes traveling gits heavy, dont it? '

The hole got done and Strutter'd peered in, half a face meshed up gainst the wall with his eye closed in on the hole to sees if she were quiet or out. Gestations be what the woman is made of...a move here or made there and if you watches close to lots, you comes to knows her: Honor Believe, sit in a old hard back chair but moved in it like it be a rocker her arms folded, a 'rocking' *within a rocker on a rock.*

What is beautiful
when a old
see's the old?

Her fingers fibbled-filled with her nose and her chin come'd rested in palms: 'He had your face but he did more fer it than you. O, not to make you feel less, it's just that he werent not you but give it a overwhelming sense of the strength of himselfs that I aint not seen in you, with your face...' She spoke her thoughts out and Strutter *seen* her voice fer the first time: '...and just if I found my imagination ...what the hell would I do with it, huh? It's way back into gone.' Honor Believe'd pull her lips to in the prune her fingers be irritated and felt fer things to touch.

Strutter, wondered on the meaning of what she be saying and since he visioned himselfs to be the object of her desire... He moved himselfs. Blinked-wiped a watering eye pushed in closer fer a better position: his shoe toe bent gainst the wall and scratched a scrape sound. It werent no importance but done took Honor Believe's attention. She raised her head toward the ceiling in response, slow at first then jerk up; so she spoke in the sky — cause she thought the sound were bove — loud and out with her eyes rolled back past her lids in her head: 'Is that you, somebody? '

Old woman you know we have to keep many
blankets about us; seems the heat be only
in our hearts these days. And we done be
caught to sleeping in our sock feet...

Lord, this woman and when we met I were ashamed as a school boy do; whistling 'hot licks' in the hallway of our place loud enough to gits some knocking on the walls fer *shushen* me and her door open'd: 'Come on in here, man. Where'd you git them licks? ' My knees buckled but I got them to git me moving toward answering her invitation. There were nothing in me but sweat and hard palpitations: 'CCCCCCan you know, I didnt no never, thinks we'd come to speak...' She shut me up with: 'Aw, I hear'd you squeaking on the bed many times...What'd you doing over there? I means alone and all...'

Strutter, lay there in disheveled bedding, grinning: 'Huh. You heard' ...and he thought on they talks of a time like when he ask her bout why she always eating nothing things and he tried to compli-please her, while Honor Believe's *mouth* be eating a piece of lettuce, a whole leaf pulled, going into...a chew at a time; the lettuce edges curled and straggly looking near crawls up her chin in scratches and Strutter, shaking his head: '...bout your weight, woman no man wants to hold a bone. But come again, no real man want to fall off a mountain he's been inspired to climb. Hell, woman! That could mess up my image; fer sho! ' The free side of Honor Believe's mouth laughs exposing no teeth there: 'Ya fool! Strutter? what the hell's kept you on this earth 'sides no place to go? ' She be still laughins, her tongue whips round her mouth then quick as quiet she'd wait as womens do receptive and pillow-face'd fer him to recover: 'My mmm, Lord lovely mind and my knowledge of women wants. Them's my abilities and the youth's is waiting to hear from *this* mind, Honey! ' She followed closely on his sayings: 'What mind, you old bastard? You been a drunk all you life. Aint no mind in you.'

Strutter's index finger and thumb pinched hair from inside a big blaring nostril of his pot marked nose: 'I gots *your* mine' and with *'mine'* on his lips he were done and sleep'd.

'...by Damn, woman!
the love fuzz, Honey, *lies...'*

Strutter put his hands together in prayer humble fashion. His elbos push them to a place near his neck and shoulder — left side — then he press lay his cheek whole head on the softness prepared of his own and sweetness of the child be in aura round him.

'...thusly ...about your face to the knoll mound which done sprouted that curls where your mouth smile *does.* Or ends. Huh! A great country field at harvest, it be, that complements the tale of life laying spread out in your yellow brown eyes. I lifts your red spotted headker-chief, that presents only your face, and expose a unkept forest. I tries hard to see the spring-gal in your tiredness ...to see the once round hips in the bone-hind of a old cow.'

Honor Believe's sound over his sound:

'O shut your mouth, Mr. Strutter.
Back on up! '

and Strutter, still in rhythm with himself, would-done-bow-way his head, smile a tiny-shy and think a dream on the last tone of Honor Believe's words:

'...go way, with yourselfs.'

the gull-birds say:
all Strutter's dreams
be made in the center
of dust ghost and last
only the blink of a eye

he dreams)

like the children
run-squeal-waddling
among the pigeons,
in scatterment

It come'd to Strutter one time when he be praying and in the middle of a coughin spell that he gots everything he'd ever wanted the day Honor Believe told she loved him and he *believed* it. And while something sure come'd right, in his mind a stir up took the meaning from the moment; left'd him on his knees plying the ground trying to find a steady and secure surface: like searching fer the *'Precious'* fer a endless time; then when finding it, not wanting to believe cause the *search* done become the *lover* but she be real and when he come'd to *believe* it *fer real,* 'I IS WHOLE,' he wished it aint never happened

now search your soul
and understand it
take more to believe
than believing sometimes

He tried not to be unthankful reached to the bottom of himselfs mumblin to a son he aint seen even in his memory lately: 'Lots of black blood fell here clot and sticken the earth to itselfs so fer you can walk on proud! '

At his fist he looked; stared on them up from where he be bent, to in the mirror but from his knees there aint no image of him show in that mirror just show'd the ceiling with its swellings and cracks. Strutter spoke to it, both: 'You laughins at me? (a strong image come'd to him) Yes. You. You laughins? Why come? I's *past* it! But you you gonna hurt. You gots the *rest* of your life to live. All I gots left to do is die. Nobody see'd me journeying here or ask: "Who I be? " Some stole to talking bout *what* I be; what I done; what I could have been but stopped cause it had no finish ...and I come'd un-noticeable.' Then he looked to the hole in the corner of his room: to *Honor Believe:* 'I locked my escape root fer you, Honey. Closed my back door and no one knows how hard that is fer a *runner* cepten the breathless.'

He closed his eyes: 'It might have been a right prettier face.'

Honor Believe mumbling to nowheres:

'I some tired, you know, fer to gits myself ready fer love. Everyone treats me with light in they eyes and closed hearts and they pain is all they willing to share. I aint even not a small notion in no bodies life just an emergency *ring* when thems that's in need make's fits and they wants they crying to be more than silence or sucked up in wall cracks 'O we come cause we know you always gonna be with us or if I aint had you...' they says all this *fallen-leaves-laughter* to me a'if I be the last limb to cling to.

'My dead sister Betty, always say: "Honor, Honey, I knows you a living help for every cause. But every man you done knowd done left you in the road surrounded by tracks, knee deep in muddy emotion spirit! Foot impressions that goes round you long side you and most walked right on over you. O woman, I haves cried for you even..." till the day she died crying, holding my hand and not wanting to leave me lone: "You done let so many people hold a burden on you and you done held up in the most way. But talk to the Lord, Honor. Talk to him. I come'd to go soon but I does it with a easy feeling the childrens, please takes care of them I knows you will." Burden! and I be ask to take care of her childrens...'

Early in the darkness of morning, he fell from his window. Layed out, mouthing the dew mist, on the ground in long dirty-white underwear bottons missing up the front looking night-naked, like the baby sparrow bird done when fell'd out from its nest in the tree. He had six hundred dollars, the mice done chew'd at the ends, clapped tween the covers in a old black leather glasses case — a rubber band clung it to his ankle. It were sometime fore we could move him and some sisters of the church and aunts — look to be sleep walking in they night clothes — done gather'd; were starting up a moan but old Aaron in a rare gum-hollow sound yell'd: 'SING OUT! yaw. I aint want to go out in no whispers' ...and trailing off ...'shit' ...

O he'd turn'd
a moving prayer
called on The Power
over his power

Old Aaron be still with us, yet a while.

Pemba,
I didn't not never go to my old man's funeral. Never stood next of his rest, didn't even see him dead — it being too late now — and so for me he aint never be gone cause I aint see'd it for me eyes. Dreams come'd so real, made me to wake and ask what city I be in — long after I moved way. When I dies, you come to see to it. You hears? So you know'd for sure so your dreams wont cause you to wake up and rush look asking questions at everything, bout WHERE YOU IS, for real or WHAT PLACE you be in and WHAT DAY IT IS? !

Aaron

EPILOGUE

I needs a rest!
O, if I could just sit
down with a pitcher of
water, look out my window over the
sea Lord!
I just needs a day

Gull-birds says: *His prayer spoken-spit over*
the plants in his window so much, the leaves
come'd of yellow-brown!

I gots my burden, you know. I wont confess it but I does sleep heavy most evenings. I use the toilet lots so I dont knows what that haves to do with it but I dont crys much any more; I just lays there in bed til I be bored with the darkness and I fergits. Sleep is to fergits I be awake. Ceptin last night I dreamed on a place of wonderment, which have a mound of grass centered and I come'd on it from out of nowheres. I wants some to cry but I be too busy: *O, I were caught to my wonderings bout this mound when some excitement come'd in me: 'SOMEONE'S COMING! '* announce *themselfs* from insides of me. Lord! 'Who says that? ' I spoke it into my hand grabbing my mouth lest I disturbs...and looked way; says: 'No matter.' I knowd somebody be coming and I wanted to see *who* this gonna be.

Well, there be a table on the mound. I looked it there. Aint inquire as to how it got...*knowd*-it-were-right- cause you gots to meet somebody somewheres: at the table; I went and stood there at the edge of the table in them spots where the grass lit light like the sun be on it.

Werent nobody there but me fer most a while then come'd lots of folks and they all got in front of me; hurryings! pushed me back til there be a people-worm formed and I be the end! Then shushens and hushens and shut-your-mouth-glares come'd from buxom-broad daughters of the church; forced the child in me to blahs out: 'But I aint says a word, Aunt Lil? '

Then I did crys, myselfs to awaken: woke with crying in my hands.

Gull-birds says:
The Lord have
straighten'd the
bended back; go
and leave your
door open

I got up and to on the warf at the lake I come'd, mumbling half things, disorder'd. In this shame – fer I regrets, Lord, talking at You like this – I be *took'd* and come'd of anger. My fist, be a old man, clutched in my falterings and clenched, trembling, to swear: *'I n-needs, damnit! Needs I ask gainst my life?'* Out of my grey, a wind, sudden'd up and be hard. Dont want no more talk ...blow'd my eyes to water; I holt'd my lips, sucked inside and bit closed gainst *it* done forced my face-way.

Something swooping spoke'd:
Aint no trouble
in the mad angry
nose of a wind;
it be a actor.
Dont be fraid

I lift'd my eyes fully-ware of my nose   taken in deep snores of breath and *blah'd* the snott sucked up on my tongue: 'BACK AT *YAH! '* leaned myselfs into the winds' blowings and Lord!   It sort of zip-inched me tall-up from my bend, rip'd my cap off my head and slapped a grey blink in my eyes with spit from the lake: but I thought I seen something!   I picked up my foot to go farward   huh-uh!   The wind stop'd my step. Put it back to where it were. *I looked at that.* The wind caught itselfs under my coat, done balloon'd and tried to pull me way   ceptin my fist kept me at a stagger til I drop'd farward and come'd to grab holt the stoop at the end of the warf: my *if's* pushed me over and it come'd to me, *I be near done come'd the distance.* I shook my head, purpose like and swallow'd whilst the wind passed over me to a *hush*   which I broken in on with my coughins: 'Water aint never been right with me. No Sir!   Grow'd-up-learnt to drink watching a dog lap at it. I aint never learnt swimming.'

My breath come'd in sniffs...   the greatest sound, til something taken my attention and *help-with-mercifulness, Lord!*   THERE!   what I seen afore, come'd-gain. It quicken'd in me: 'Mercy be alive! ' I stood. Weak; fergetful of the *else*   believing, but: 'Aw, it caint be.' I wipe'd water from my grin where my eyes flow'd: 'SON!   Goddamnit. It you, aint it? '

'Where you git the boat from? What?

'What you doings on the lake?

'Come on in here, boy! Yeah. Huh.'

I waved in his comings; shuck with laughins. And he done. In slows. He done it. Son, row'd up to the warf... I be a stutter; too much this-to-that and: 'Hurry, boy.' He looked some like I felt of myselfs and I firm *knowd* his talkings, called out cone-like: *'Old man? Come. Git in. We gon fishing.'* 'Yeah. Un-huh,' was in my nods.

Light busted on me like the highest *'E'* sound in a fiddle and a stomp of gospel pushed me farward; I squinted and up'd my hand to shade my seeings —dont want to loose no sight of, Son— But *'the swooping'* come'd, flew over, let some drop-leavings to land in the dip tween my thumb and next finger. It yelled at me. The damn'd bird yelled at me:

'I needs'
can be your
helps gainst
receivings

I: 'Damn! ' grab'd at the gull-bird; slip'd... Son's boat give — *I went down there in the autumn rust mongst the leaves and sun-caused-steam: make me to looks, stretched out there, like I be something cooking! Aunt Lil, whoop-shouting through the screen door: 'Boy, you just like a stomp on the kitchen floor when the bread be rising. Git out o' the mud! '*

Then a Presence come'd on me. O it were holy, un-shape'd, tho, shapen in me feelings of fergiveness and *'dont care'd'* what I done or was, just love: flown free. I come'd a joy. I wanted to talks to it and *it* come'd a face with long slow-moving white hair, taking turns to the left and right, and a white beard: a great snowing around His deep blue eyes stuck in a olive selfs. But my mouth wont talks. He have eyes of solution, that be like my words: happy and sad at the same time, then even not *there* and ifn I stares long enough, He looked like everybody I done really knowd and after'd I done lost whatever be wrong. Fergot my questions.

A 'follow me' feeling were what caused a movement stirring in me and He reached grab'd my hand tightly and run'd with me right up through the light at the top of the water. I come'd up, well then course, as I been'd baptised: bobbin like rubber and I grab'd a green rope tied at the stump-post; went down again but pulled myselfs up; crawled cussing on to the warf. Son, swim'd over calling at me: I says I be alright, just got some damn water in my nose. Are you alright? He climb'd, shaking *'yes's'* onto the side of the warf and catched him some breath then went back into the water to git the boat. I stood, looked at my wetness and sit down. There were talking I sure it be the Lord and I rested into a *rocking myselfs.* The voice spoke from the 'WHERES': Ever We wants you. You can spits on it.' I bow'd, Yes Sir.

Son brung the boat over to the warf, come'd on and sit near next of me. Again: 'You alright? ' and I smiled it fatherly back at him and we be awhile just staring; stare-looked at each other hard! and started laughins. I looked off, up to finds that gull-bird, son of a— Son says: 'Old man? Somebody will come and git you.' and when I turned back he were *gone.* But I trust him. I be waiting here fer somebody, just like he says soon they comings.

Old Strutter's bald
head, peaked tween
some lake weed and viewed

from over, you might
says, fer sure – you
see'd a full head of

hair
flowing
as the waves

The gull-birds with twisted necks continued from under they wings:

Mae-lulu
Mae-lulu!
Snow dolphins it were — look; see —
dragging

Mae-lulu
Mae-lulu!
the Strutter
been fell'd
to the sand
they laid 'im

Mae-lulu
Mae-
          lulu...

from in
a tear